## ADVANCE PRAISE FOR MERCY GENE

Brilliant and heart-searing, *Mercy Gene* is about what it means to be ensnared by others' hard definitions of who you are as you desperately try to stay inside a brain, a body, a life. With the insight and charisma of a god, Derbyshire undresses language to get to the very marrow of their experience. Their wisdom is the rare kind that comes from the dangerous and costly brink-of-sanity, brink-of-death view. As I read, I wanted to slow myself down so I could spend more time inside their perfect, sonic sentences. Derbyshire writes radiantly and hilariously from the padded rooms, the crawl spaces, the edges of the known world. Theirs is a fierce and beautiful account of what it means to be an artist, a mother, and a human when you cannot be drawn or, too often, even seen inside the lines. A supernova of a book, to read *Mercy Gene* is to be changed by it.

—Claudia Dey, author of *Heartbreaker*

The DNA of *Mercy Gene* is a dizzying double helix of creative gusto, funhouse humour, hard-won wisdom, and ferocious empathy. After reading Derbyshire's *sui generis* autofiction, I was on bended knees—not pleading for mercy but begging for more of their trail-blazing truth-telling. *Mercy Gene* will set minds and hearts afire.

— Zsuzsi Gartner, author of *The Beguiling*

*Mercy Gene* is an incredible book that lifted me right up off the ground and away to other places both hard and soft. It's essential reading for anyone wanting to know what the agony of psychic pain is really like, but it's also very funny. Thank you, thank you to JD for this ferocious, devastating and illuminating, tender and vulnerable, mountain peak and universal embrace of a book and for being in the world. Exquisite.

— Miriam Toews, author of *Fight Night*

*Mercy Gene* is a book to carry with you forever. Like a smooth and lucky stone in your pocket, or a poem you memorized so you could always read it back to yourself. So much of this prose is pure poetry. Lists, quips, quotes, and micro stories cross-stitched into a shifty masterpiece that tells us the unadorned true story of one person's dance with mental health, pharmaceuticals, and themself.

—Ivan Coyote, author of *Care Of*

JD DERBYSHIRE

# MERCY GENE

### THE MAN-MADE MAKING
### OF A MAD WOMAN

GOOSE LANE

Edited by Bethany Gibson.
Copy edited by John Sweet.
Cover concept by JD Derbyshire and Dana Ayotte. Graphics by Julie Scriver.
Page design by Julie Scriver.
"Luka," words and music by Suzanne Vega, © 1987 WC Music Corp. and Waifersongs Ltd. All rights administered by WC Music Corp. All rights reserved. Used by permission of Alfred Music.
Printed in Canada by Marquis.
10 9 8 7 6 5 4 3 2 1


Library and Archives Canada Cataloguing in Publication

Title: Mercy gene : the man-made making of a mad woman / J.D. Derbyshire.
Names: Derbyshire, J.D., author.
Identifiers: Canadiana (print) 20220405468 | Canadiana (ebook) 20220408769 | ISBN 9781773102948 (softcover) | ISBN 9781773102955 (EPUB)
Classification: LCC PS8607.E7155 M43 2023 | DDC C813/.6—dc23


Goose Lane Editions acknowledges the generous support of the Government of Canada, the Canada Council for the Arts, and the Government of New Brunswick.

Goose Lane Editions is located on the unceded territory of the Wǝlastǝkwiyik whose ancestors along with the Mi'kmaq and Peskotomuhkati Nations signed Peace and Friendship Treaties with the British Crown in the 1700s.

Goose Lane Editions
500 Beaverbrook Court, Suite 330
Fredericton, New Brunswick
CANADA E3B 5X4
gooselane.com

à la folie

Sorry Ma'am. I was dreaming that I was awake.
That should count for something shouldn't it?

　—Peppermint Patty

## Like this

It happens like this, in fragments that come out of order, unruly, sudden, begging to be seen, like older drunk women dressed up for a night on the town. A mess of images, half-formed and slippery, sometimes shouting, "Don't forget me," then disappearing quickly, blurs in a downpour of black-and-white words, just like that.

## Me Ma Me Ma Me Ma

Crisis is emergency in drag. For decades there was a small red light flashing in the distance from a point in time that would one day no longer be the past. I was aware of it in my peripheral vision, on and off like one of those floaters you get in your eyes as you age. One day, the flashing red light was suddenly in front of me, perched on top of an ambulance. I understood it was the ambulance that should have been called to the scene of a crime when Janice was thirteen years old. It was twenty-eight years late and I was no longer Janice, but I got in and the ambulance took me away.

## Rules of engagement 1

Some people know me as Jan Derbyshire. I prefer JD. My parents are still partial to Janice. I chopped the *ice* off Janice in grade nine. Everyone was fine with that except my parents and the government. I would have chopped *nice* off the end, but that would have left me as simply *Ja*, yes in German. I didn't think I could pull that off. I had a nickname as a kid on sports teams and with friends. JD. It's what I use now. Outwardly, JD works as my initials. Inwardly, I know JD stands for my true name, Joshua Dandelion, a genderqueer, lesbian woboy who can make the sun stop in its tracks and is seen as a weed but has incredibly useful properties. JD wrote this book for Janice and Jan.

## We Ma We Ma We Ma

We arrived with some passing sirens, caught a free ride on the windy wail of sound waves, screeching like off-key cats learning opera. No one knew we were there. A perfect hiding spot, an auditory camouflage keeping us secret long enough to make it to the next brain that was ours to possess.

You gotta love this man-made yet unearthly sound. Intended to attract attention—clear the way, emergency, emergency, stop everything, let us through—so commanding. All to arrive as quickly as possible at the scene of a human failing of one sort or another. This sound can never mean anything good, although we've learned that, for some humans, a siren, like the ringing of a bell for a good Buddhist, can bring a person back to the here and now. A siren can remind poor humans how soft they really are, and that at any given moment they could run into something hard and non-negotiable. A siren brings them back to themselves because someone else just broke. Gratitude kisses their thoughts like morning dew, refreshes everything, clears the clutter, and triggers the giving of thanks for simple things: walking down the street with all their bits in their right places, everything going tickety-boo, this body, for today, is complete, untorn, miraculous in how the bits work together. The senses sense. The nose smells the scent of a freshly sprayed dandelion patch, the mouth still tastes that last swill of coffee, swallowed in a rush, the hands brush toast crumbs off the cotton pants, the eyes track the ambulance as it passes by, the ears listen to the fading sound of an emergency moving farther and farther away from them and smack into the life of someone else.

Poor humans and their constant banging about, accidental by nature, so easily distracted, so clumsy. Thin bags of blood and bone and soft organs, like wounded gazelles watching lions get closer and closer, waiting in the shade for their inevitable demise.

Even the biggest and strongest of the human men and women—and everything in between—are flowers; delicate, crushable flowers. And here we speak only of the body. Don't get us started on the brain, which is designed, it seems, to break. It would have been more honest to make it out of glass. Then the poor humans would have half a chance of understanding how easily it can be damaged, how unavoidable chips and cracks are, and how high the odds really are of shattering the poor little sucker to smithereens. The thing should be covered in stickers: Fragile, Fragile, Seriously, This Side Up, Really Fucking Fragile! Don't shake, don't stir, don't bang about, don't hit, don't fill with too many abstract ideas. Poor humans, so vulnerable, so obsessed with pretending not to be. Badly designed from the beginning, whenever that was.

Oh, they have their theories, they love their theories. When you think about evolution, for example, and we don't mean deeply, we just mean when you think about that one idea about the retaining and strengthening of traits most favourable to survival in a species, and then you look at humans, how can you not say, "What the fuck, this is what made it through?"

And then there's our sneaking suspicion that these glass-brained bags of blood lean toward self-destruction. They've built a world of haves and have-nots surrounded by metal and concrete and glass and guns, fucking guns and bombs and chemicals and lest we forget, contact sports. They seem driven to make things up that hurt themselves. Including us. We are auditory hallucinations, we are not from the realm of hard realities, we are delusional. And we come from somewhere we don't even know.

On the day we arrived, inside the passing sirens, we flew into the narrow ear canals of a thirteen-year-old girl. It was the spring of 1974, and it was you. You, Janice, dishevelled and confused behind some faded-green grain elevator in southern Alberta.

You had no idea that it wasn't just broken beer-bottle glass at your feet. You had dropped your brain. And that's how we got in, the voices in your head.

## And the doctors said

There was a man there, running his fingers over my head. He beeped out loud. Beep Beep Beep. He said he was a psychiatrist, but I knew the truth. He was the mental detector. He was searching for buried treasures in my head. And oh, the treasures he found. Beep. Here are some of the psychiatric labels affixed to me between 2000 and 2005: Beep. Alcoholism—fair enough; Beep. Beep. Auditory hallucinations—two for two. I have heard voices since I was thirteen. Then there was Beep, beep, beep; depression, general anxiety disorder, and Complex PTSD. Then came, Beep. Gender identity disorder, you can't get that one anymore, thank you Trans Nation. Followed by Beep, beep, beep beep beep; bipolar affective disorder 2, bipolar 1, bipolar 1 rapid cycling, ADHD, schizoaffective disorder, and, for a short and terrifying time, BEEP! Schizophrenia.

I didn't have them all at the same time. It seems each doctor who treated me needed a diagnosis to fit my story into, so we wouldn't have to go through my whole story every single time. Their diagnosis became my story. And in the midst of all that, I really didn't know what my story was, so I bought their book. The *Diagnostic and Statistical Manual*, 4th Edition. Number of pages, 886. Number of diagnoses, 297. What a read. I'd never heard stories told like that, so medical, so certain. I did wonder where the parts of me that didn't fit into the doctors' way of telling went. Those pesky tangential thoughts, my mother's maiden name, the half-cooked unremembered, the starts of poems, the formula for aerodynamics, the piles of untold secrets tied together like stacks of old newspapers in the attic, the run-on sentences limping badly, the words to the Big Mac jingle, the facts and fictions merging into factions, the blur of memories surfacing like milk-soaked photographs, the phone numbers for dead people. Did my brain have a Tickle Trunk somewhere, like Mr. Dressup had? Was everything the doctors didn't have time for locked inside? Did my amygdala swallow the key? Would I be able to get to it again when I needed it? I tried not to think about it too much. The drugs helped. Antipsychotics are like that. You start thinking of the beginning of a sentence in your head and then it stops; you can't find the end. You are a dog on a leash-free trail that doesn't know where to run.

I came to appreciate the brevity of diagnosis, like the Coles Notes of personal tragedy, handy melt-in-your-mouth plot and theme summaries that I could offer to people who asked. I'm Bipolar or I have Complex PTSD, so many candy-covered chocolates in the pack. Not many people wanted the full story anyway, and even if they did, I wasn't sure I could tell it. Was it a comedy or a tragedy? Aren't most stories both? And stories are almost always told one of two ways: a guy becomes a hero or a hero becomes just a guy. Mr. Aristotle and his hero's journey: life as is, something happens that's going to change everything, you go through a series of increasingly difficult obstacles that seem impossible to get through, but you do, or you don't, and then there's one last push, a big climax. Then it's all over, denouement. (Snore)

It's so like sex as it is for men. I'm curious about what it would be like if Mrs. Aristotle had been in charge of outlining how we tell a good story. Perhaps she would have suggested that we tell stories like sex as it is for women. Fun fact: sex can be very different for women every time. Women can have that one big climax like men have, or a little climax, or a bunch of climaxes in various sizes and intensities. Sometimes women have surprise climaxes. Didn't see that one coming. Sometimes the story is finished and it's so unsatisfying that we have to make up our own ending.

### Known triggers (1)

A million shades of green
Jelly beans in a jar
Clichés about sewing
The distance between $x$ and $y$
Clinging to perfection
Blood to the mouth
Old aging pain
Bodies of dead sentences
Ants that listen
The name Janice
Liver and onions
Oil furnaces
A day a lot like this one
Waiting for the space in a conversation
Morphine-like hormones
Heart-shaped things

## What the fuck happened?

The first time I was hospitalized and certified insane was a surprise to everyone, including me. I was sitting in my apartment on a grey couch with orange pillows. I was eating toast with honey. I was drinking tea. I thought it was just another day. True, thoughts, ideas, and feelings were flying over my corpus callosum like cows gone mad in an endlessly repeated nursery rhyme. And, for no apparent reason, "Hey diddle diddle. Hey diddle diddle," echoed throughout my cerebellum. There was a cat playing fiddle in my right frontal lobe and a good sport of a dog laughing and pissing up and down my brain stem. For culinary reasons that were clearly outside sanity's protocol, a dish running away with a spoon fell out of my ear and clattered to the ground. The fork and the knife remained in my brain, gleaming for the attention they felt they deserved. "Avoid sharp, pointy things," one of the airborne bovines reminded me on her last pass over the mood. This piece of advice made the most sense to me as trillions of synapses and snippets of sayings and opinions and trivia fought to be heard in my head. It was a cerebral dog's breakfast, brought to me by Kellogg's: Snap, Crackle, and Pop. Logic played hide-and-seek in the lateral ventricles, rage riots broke out in the pituitary gland, and moments were stolen indiscriminately, from every lobe. Outside my window, the grass began to growl, I could hear a squirrel's heartbeat, the leaves on the cherry trees screamed green. The emotional roller coaster kept on going. A carny, hanging out in my hypothalamus, yelled, "Do you want to go faster?" I heard myself answer, "Fuck, yesssssss!"

I flew off my amusement park moorings, overshot the sound of mind completely, and landed in the street with nothing but a pack of cigarettes and a rant. I started batting Starbucks coffee cups out of people's hands, denouncing them all as addicts of North America's most insidious drug, coffee. I popped up on a metal newspaper box and began to pontificate on the evils of caffeine.

*Caffeine does not give you energy. It stimulates your nervous system, and that's not energy, that's stress. The energy you get from caffeine is on loan from your adrenals and your liver, and the interest you pay is high—anxiety, depression, hypertension, hypoglycemia, mood disorders— so give it up. Starfucks, Starfucks, Starfucks.*

I knocked coffee cups out of people's hands—in— slow—motion.

It was sort of like that, from what I can remember. I vividly recall what happened next. Some lovely boys in blue came (police?), put a lovely pair of locking bracelets on my wrists (handcuffs?). They put me gently into the back of their pumpkin (squad car?) and took me to the ball (hospital?). I was admitted against my will. (Certified?)

—sung to the tune of "The Girl from Ipanema"

Lithium adds some Zyprexa
Seroquel twinned with Effexor
Risperdal, Zyban, and Prozac too.

Wellbutrin, Xanax, and Paxil
Tegretol and Chlorpromazine
Olanzapine, Ativan, and Celexa.

Oh, what a wonderful feeling.
To hit an emotional ceiling.
Never too high or too low.
Numbed out with nowhere to go.

—and repeat

## Land of rape and honey

Where did the idea to do what they did come from? Movies, magazines, porn, big talk from other guys? Six or seven in a pickup truck, farm boys, in grades eleven and twelve, they boasted to Janice, didn't they? What's that? Sixteen and seventeen, a little older for the dumb ones. Not even thick enough to throw the shadow of a man. What the fuck?

Maybe the idea came from the cropped fields blanketed up against the highway that went through town. Rapeseeds carried on the wind, floating through their open bedroom windows to nestle in their still-downy ear hairs. Lying in wait for the perfect combination of beer and darkness and a down-to-earth girl with a mound ripe for planting. Rape flowers in July, yellow for the cowards that did what they did in the spring. Bees love rape flowers, plenty of nectar to be sucked, but the honey is harsh and peppery and has to be sold as bakery grade or mixed with a milder variety to even begin to come close to sweet. Rape honey is hard to swallow. Maybe that's why they started calling it sexual assault.

## Lament: a passionate expression of grief or sorrow

*As far as I could tell, stories may enable us to live, but they also trap us, bring us spectacular pain. In their scramble to make sense of nonsensical things, they distort, codify, blame, aggrandize, restrict, omit, betray, mythologize, you name it. This has always struck me as a cause for lament, not celebration.*

— Maggie Nelson, *The Argonauts*

I'm not entirely sure it happened. Maybe I made up everything. I have no solid evidence. Maybe I've been doing nothing but wasting time, trying to put together one big, sad lie of a movie in the little dark room that is my head. I should be out there learning to play Frisbee golf or volunteering at the food bank, but I often get stuck on my couch for days, obsessed. I endlessly review fragmented clips, often unfocused, rarely miked properly, mostly out of sync. Sometimes a scene comes to me, complete and beautiful, but I don't know where it belongs in the film.

Like the one shot on that lake in northern Ontario where they'd all gone to visit French-Canadian relatives. Yes, there were fiddles and clog dancing and drinking, lots of drinking, and everybody's Export "A" packs getting mixed up.

Men missing teeth but not afraid to laugh with wide-open mouths, and big women, bigger than Janice had ever seen, eating pie and double burgers and scoop after scoop of potato salads. In some cousin's cabin, curtains of beige and brown and green, hunters with dogs, and guns aimed at the sky full of ducks flying away—this pattern repeated over the length of the curtains, on the lining of the sleeping bags, and on the homemade cushions tied to the bench seats in the aluminum boat.

A boat with a little engine that putts them out to the middle of the lake.

It turns out Janice had a knack for fishing. She easily wormed the hook, and when she dropped the line, sharp-toothed, skinny pikes came to her, one after the other, until she'd caught eight fish and the others in the boat, the boys, caught none. When they putt-putted back to shore for lunch, her father commandingly suggested that she not return to fishing in the afternoon. He sealed the deal by putting a dollar in her hand. Janice didn't understand. Her father said she should give the boys a chance. The boys looked back at Janice and her dad. They seemed to know that she was being kicked off the boat for being good at fishing. She was not supposed to be angry, but she was. She bought ten Crispy Crunch chocolate bars with the dollar and ate them one after the other, high up in a tree, where she tried to send messages to the pike not to let the boys catch them. When they came back in, there were no fish, and Janice began to believe that she had secret powers that she would have to be careful with. Her father taught her how to clean the fish. When they slit the belly of one, eggs spilled out and her father said, "You killed a lot of fish today." Why did he say *kill*? She thought they'd talked about what they did to fish as *caught*. She got through gutting the fish and then went and puked behind the cabin. She didn't think it was about the blood and entrails and that tang of dead and lake. Maybe, but she blamed the Crispy Crunch bars combined with the guilt of knowing she was now a killer. Later that night, the drunk, grown-up cousins took the unlucky fisher boys down to the dock, where they shone flashlights on the water. The pike swarmed to the surface in such great numbers they scooped them out with nets. They won, but they cheated.

You learn to give up your place in the boat without a fight, you learn to follow rules even though others cheat, you learn to eat chocolate bars to stuff the anger down. Maybe that's why all the women there were so big, Janice thought. They weren't allowed in the boats anymore.

## Ticket to ride

Every time I left the psychiatric ward, I felt as though I was wearing a pharmaceutical straitjacket that no one could see. The arms-pinned-across-the-chest-and-tied-off-at-the-back white jackets had fallen out of fashion, at least in the public eye. The preferred method, then and now, is to bind the mind with drugs. The meds slam the door shut on emotional sensations, disappear deep thinking, nullify decision-making, and erase any inklings of curiosity. A "Do Not Disturb Any Further" sign is often mistaken for a pouting lower lip.

They give you free bus tickets when you leave the hospital and a list of drop-in centres and soup kitchens, but most of them don't open till nine or ten. So, I rode the Davie bus, through downtown and then to the ocean. I saw glass buildings and ribbons of people. I felt incredibly late for some gigantic party I hadn't been invited to. The bus smelled of other people's feet. I smelled like hospital food. Not much of a difference really. I couldn't help mumbling words of encouragement to myself, *Everything's fine, everything's fine*. My short-term memory was shot. I couldn't remember what I used to do for a living. When the bus returned to the Stanley Park loop for the third time, the driver suggested I go for a walk and try singing to the birds.[1]

---

1    Please reference page 21 for the song I sang.

It wasn't all bad. I was calmer, and the voices were gone. Unfortunately, I experienced an incredibly difficult side effect. Suddenly, I thought about wanting to die, all the time. The doctors called it suicidal ideation. Previously, I had thought of side effects as something small and inconsequential, like itchy knees or bum pimples. You know, like a side salad with your main meal. But wanting to kill yourself 24-7, that's not a side salad, that's a whole side of beef beside your plate of roast beef. That's big! And who decides these things? *These are the main effects, and these are the side effects.* Isn't an effect an effect? When you say it's a side effect, it makes it sound as if it's going to happen *near* you, not *in* you. If you take a pill that makes you gain weight, the fat will just pile up beside you, and you can leave it there when you go out, just call the fat sitter. But suicidal ideation? What the fuck?

## Known triggers (2)

Small moths
Abandoned drive-ins
Sea cucumbers
Anyone named Bill
Greek myths
Fruit leather
Pinch-hitters
Smirks on children
Father's Day cards that feature cavemen
Betty Crocker
Town criers
When Tony Robbins says, "Get juiced"

## Peanuts, pop porn, and Cracker Jacks

So hear this, from the things in her head that arrived uninvited to nestle in her ears, pink with the blush of a slightly embarrassed thirteen-year-old girl. She is not beautiful enough to have been imagined by Nabokov, not even close. Janice was more likely to have been conjured by Charles M. Schulz, Peppermint Patty, but slipped out of those Birkenstock sandals and into Converse Chuck Taylor high-tops. She could be called Jellybean Janice.

Schulz sketching, maybe, on a deadline for the dailies, swivels on his metallic-grey industrial stool at his over-sized drawing board. Possibly distracted by the smells of spring, he turns toward the window to see the ducks on the pond frolicking in the sunshine. He doesn't give a second thought to the little girl he's just drawn, all alone in a cartoon panel without a speech bubble above her head or anything.

Something about the way the drake holds the duck's head under water while he mounts her from behind shakes loose some fact in Schulz's head that he'd heard somewhere but was trying to forget.

One out of four women in North America will be sexually assaulted, most in their early teens. And those are just the ones who tell. What crosses Schulz's mind is a long line of young almost-women, Lolita leading the charge, just after she became something that had to be had. He is curious. Why do some men still say things like, "I had to have it, I had to do it," as if it's a matter of inevitability that every girl who pops from a blossom into a cherry on the tree has to be picked?

Schulz takes a sip of his Nescafé instant coffee, cold hours ago in his cup. He's trembling. He realizes how little he actually knows about drawing a young girl like this. And with that tremble, the ink pot spilled onto the page, gathering into a smudge of black that pooled around Jellybean Janice's feet faster than prairie rain clouds can tumble out of nowhere to change the mood of a perfectly sunny day. As the ink soaked into the paper, Schulz watched Jellybean Janice disappear into this little bit of something gone wrong and wondered what he could have done differently. Then Schulz went to bed to spoon his wife and vowed to draw another little girl in the morning. That's how Peppermint Patty came to be. Schulz even drew her a special friend, Marcie, for when Patty grew weary of the boys and Lucy. Schulz also swore off reading literature by certain men.

## Chronic female

It could have been so much worse. I was living beyond the lifetimes of women like Virginia Woolf or Zelda Fitzgerald or Frances Farmer or Sylvia Plath or Charlotte Perkins Gilman, or T.S. Eliot's wife, what was her name? Oh well, the point being, if you spared the wife, you'd spoil the poet. And who could keep track of the hordes of Freudian-slip-wearing women deemed hysterical for the mad act of trying to tell the truth of their experiences? I didn't load my pockets with rocks and walk into a river. I wasn't sent away and locked up for good. I wasn't lobotomized. I didn't stick my head in a gas oven. I didn't let the yellowing wallpaper convince me that I was better off dead. If it had been even thirty years earlier, I might have been committed to the Riverview psychiatric facility in Coquitlam, BC. The building where women were kept was called the Female Chronic Unit. I've seen pictures showing attendants carrying the drugs up to the women in ice cream buckets. The Female Chronic Unit. I mean, they wouldn't have been wrong. I am a "long-suffering woman," a female, chronic unit. FCU!

Fuck U.

# A memo possibly dictated by the voices

We love to bring the noise, squeaky wheels, frat boys, street buskers. We bring it, 24-7, the sound of mind, crackling over your brain waves. Smirk now while this tiny blob of semi-sweet lucidity makes some sort of sense. Listen to you trying to find words to make this somehow understandable to someone outside yourself. Ha ha, trim the sails, trim the fat, liposuction out the tear tear terror of what we really are. What the fuck? What's the skinny? Are you really trying to Disney us? Us? Voices that would burn the ears off Mickey Mouse. Not to mention Howard Fucking Stern. King Baby Man himself. Fucking piss shit piece of garbage twat fucking loser shithead. (This is the Disney version.) And yes, Twat. We still say Twat. Blame too many British comedians. Even if you told. The truth. HBO wouldn't touch this story with a ten-foot pole. Do they even have a ten-foot pole? Maybe on one of their subsidiary porn channels. That's where all the money is, and all the poles. Stop fucking fishing. We make no sense. Stop attempting to explain us to yourself, to others. You'll never get it down. You can't catch us.

There's a big gaping hole in your word net, you idiot. The work of language is to be rational. We're not that, never that. We exist to fuck you up, fuck you over, fucking fuck fuck. Write, write, write the wrongs. Ha Ha Fucking

Ha. Parade around in your inky swimsuit, represent Miss Understood. All those little stories you tell yourself, about how all of this will eventually make sense. Fucking hilarious. Collecting the famous voice hearers of history, the ones you've heard about that did some good. Do you think Joan of Arc just heard about attacking the British, or that Anthony Hopkins's little voices only criticized his Shakespearean acting, or that Carl Jung and Philip K. Dick just had dream stories that id and ego told to them in a lovely linear logic that they just had to write down?

Do you really believe that John Nash, tortured by brilliance and, oh yeah, vicious, vicious voices, actually ignored the nasty shit and focused only on the answers to all his mathematical problems? Who knows what unreported utterances lurked in the minds of the famous. Who cares?

You are fucked. Frog in boiling water fucked, galaxy-sucking black hole fucked, looking for an abortion in America Fucked. Fucked. Fucked. Fucked. We will always be here. Fucking you up, you dumb fuck. Chew on this fuck for a minute: all suicides are assisted suicides. And the final fuck will be sudden. There will be an unguarded moment, a tear in the gossamer veil of vigilance you've mistaken for armour. And what we tell you to fucking do, you will fucking do. We will take your fucking life, but everyone will think it was you who took it. That's how fucking good we are.

## The interviews

Almost all the psychiatrists I had were older white men with terrible ties and no sense of humour. They were all bald except for one little man with red cones of hair on the sides of his head. He looked like Krusty the Clown, which didn't help. None of them were into small talk; they would just dive right in. The interviews were tense because I knew they were looking for something that was wrong with me and that they would be the ones deciding what was wrong. I was nervous and couldn't find the right words, so I'd improvise. I'd say yes to anything that popped into my head and let it out of my mouth. Which is a great skill to have onstage playing theatresports at Loose Moose, but not a wise thing to do during a psychiatric interview. FYI.

**First doctor**
*Why do you dress like a boy, Janice?*

Please call me Jan. These aren't boys' clothes, they're on me, so they're my clothes. Boy oh boy oh boy. Boyish. I can see that. Some of the best things about me are kind of considered boyish. I'm curious, adventurous, and I have a bouncy intellect, but I know I'm not a real boy, Dr. Geppetto.

**Next doctor**

*Would you consider yourself a tomboy, Janice?*

Please call me Jan. What does that even mean, Tomboy? What can I tell you? I was born in Calgary, a beautiful, pink, bouncing baby girl. It was a miracle. A Hi-Bounce Pinky. A beautiful bouncing baby girl. It's not just baby boys who bounce, Doc. I used to tell a joke in my stand-up act. "When I was growing up, I was a Tomboy; now, I'm a Tomman."

Don't worry, Doc, there's so many things you real men can do that we will never be able to do. Real men can write their names in the snow.

**Next doctor**

*Were you a disappointment to your parents, Janice?*

It's Jan and yes, I was. Isn't everybody?

*How would you have won your parents' approval?*

I don't know. I think I would have stayed in Calgary. I'd be a Special Education teacher, you know. I'd work with the special ones, K–3. I'd live in Lake Bonavista in a baby-blue bungalow I bought with my hu, hu—sorry, this is hard for me to get out. My husband, um…Donny. He's dead now. He died seven years ago; Calgary Stampede, too much tequila. My God, he was trying to fuck some princess in a cowboy hat on a mechanical bull. But oh, how I'd loved that bad man.

I still remember the first time he asked me to line dance at the Ranchman's Bar and Grill on McLeod Trail. He told me I was beautiful. And I said, Well, come here, you broken, fucked-up man.

Let's make love.

Let's get married.

Let's fall deeply into tragedy and explode into a cacophony of feathers because we were the stupid chickens that didn't hear the shotgun at the wedding.

Oh well, time passes, might as well make the best of things.

Chicken pot pie?

Not hungry, Doctor?

**Next doctor**

*What do you think about beauty, Janice?*

Okay. How about a haiku? Haiku for you, Doctor?

Beauty is an ass
Licking hobo that's not all
she's cracked up to be.

Wow. What? I'm not sure where that came from?

Let me try again, Doctor.

Beauty is in the eye of the beer holder. Glib. I know, I know, I know. Beauty is as beauty does?

Oh shit. Wait. Beauty is…commitment!

What you see is 125,000 dollars (US) of commitment to this body, because I believe in myself.

I'm a capital W woman.

You can have any body you want now. There are no more excuses.

We have the plastics.

If you scramble up the letters in the word *beauty*, you get *eat* and *buy*.

Don't eat, and buy yourself a body, a good one.

**Next doctor**
*Why do you hate being a woman, Janice?*

I don't hate being a woman. There are all kinds of women. I just happen to be this kind. I hate what happened to me because I'm a woman.

*Have you thought about how different your life would be if you were a man?*

Sure, who hasn't? It doesn't mean I want to be one. I mean, maybe if I could pick what kind. If I could choose, I'd be a big man, like offensive-lineman big, and not the CFL, the NFL. I'd be a big man who talked a little like this:

My name is Haus. I'm big and I got guns. I got guns in my boots. I got guns in my bum. That's right, I got guns up my bum.

Little tiny bum guns. You can't even see those little tiny bum guns in metal detectors, that's how tiny those little tiny bum guns are.

I got guns on my head, mounted right on my hat.

I drive around in my truck, listening to Patsy Cline, and I thank the Lord Jesus that I ain't no helpless woman. I'm big and I got guns. If you get up in my grille, I'll put a hole in you.

**Last doctor**
*No more questions.*

## Hi-Bounce Pinky

You see a person walk down the street bouncing a pink rubber ball. You think this is crazy, or a simple *hmm* escapes from your lips. If you think this is crazy, you cross the street and carry on with your day. If you think *hmm*, you get closer. You see that although the person is wearing a hoodie and a ball cap, you can't tell if it's a man or a woman. You think this is crazy or this is interesting. If you think this is crazy, you cross the street and carry on with your day. If you think this is interesting, you watch as they stop to bounce the ball off a brick wall. You step closer and see that they're an older person, maybe even in their fifties. You think this is crazy or this is different. If you think this is crazy, you cross the street and carry on with your day. If you think this is different, you wait. They see you see them. They stop bouncing the ball. They offer you the ball. You think this is crazy or this is curious. If you think this is crazy, you cross the street and carry on with your day. If you think this is curious, you extend your hand. They place the pink bouncy ball in your hand.

You think this is crazy or this is inviting. If you think this is crazy, you give the ball back, cross the street, and carry on with your day. If you think this is inviting, you feel a pink rubber bouncy ball in your hand for the first time in a long time, maybe ever. You bounce the rubber ball on the cement. You catch it. You smile. You try to hand the pink rubber ball back to the person who gave it to you. They tell you to keep it and walk away.

You are now the person walking down the street bouncing a pink rubber bouncy ball. But then you remember all the things that could happen if you drop the ball. People who drop the ball lose their jobs or their partners or their kids or any opportunity they might have had. It all falls to shit when you drop the ball. You pocket the ball, cross the street, and carry on with your day.

## Rules of engagement 2

People are always telling stories to themselves about themselves. Some stories are someone else's telling. Some of these stories need to be rewritten, some of these stories need to be abandoned at the side of the road. Some of us need to change our name to leave behind the stories we don't want to carry anymore. When you're Queer, it's no big deal to change your name or to have different names for different stories. Queer people also change their pronouns without much of a kerfuffle. We change pronouns and then change them back, sometimes we make up names for our pronouns or invent new ones. Most of my life, however, is spent in predominantly straight and gender-conforming spaces and places. Begrudgingly, in these spaces, to represent the idea of possibilities, JD uses the pronouns *they/them* because it's all they've got. Both Janice and Jan used *she/her*. The truth is, I haven't found language that fits, but I have found clothes that fit, so that's something.

## Form follows function

Grain elevators are usually 70 to 120 feet tall. They were designed to receive, store, and ship grain in bulk. In 1923, French architect Le Corbusier hailed the grain elevator's stark and simple geometric shape as the ultimate example of form following function.

To be clear: A truck from a farm, loaded with grain, stops on a scale outside the grain elevator. The truck is weighed and continues to the work floor. Grain is dumped from the rear of the truck and falls into a pit, where it is moved upward by a continuous belt with flat-backed buckets attached. The grain is then directed to bins by a long spout. The truck is again driven across the scale and weighed a second time to determine how much grain was unloaded. The farmer is told the weight and can sell the grain right away or pay a storage fee to hold the grain and sell it later.

All grain elevators were utilitarian buildings, and so specific that when they weren't needed anymore, the form ceased to function. The small, windowless, sloping compartments were difficult to convert into anything useful. Even salvaging the wood was impossible because it was so old, hard, and riddled with metal spikes that it was more like concrete. The grain elevators served only to house teenaged drinkers and all their shenanigans: parties, heavy metal music, graffiti, rapes, pillages, etc. Town councils voted to have them torn down.

People mourned the disappearance of the grain elevators, sometimes nicknamed prairie cathedrals. But JD was delighted when the icons of the prairie began to go. From a dreamlike distance, JD watched them fall, little charms on a bracelet of bad luck coming off and getting lost, and with the disappearance of these souvenirs, JD hoped all the bad memories of that time on the prairies would be forgotten.

Years later, JD decided to drive there, looking forward to seeing them gone. But in Nanton, a town about an hour south of Calgary, three grain elevators, now richly painted and converted into a museum and an art gallery, stood tall. As soon as JD saw them ruining the wide open space of the prairies, any sense of time and distance they'd hoped to hang on to between where they were now and what had happened then began to collapse with the sound of farmers' sons laughing and grunting and coughing up centuries of grain dust impossible to get rid of.

## Brrrs

Ideas take longer than statues to topple. They stick to us, like burrs in the bloodstream. Even when we think we've let go, moved on, reconsidered, agreed to a necessary and complete transfusion to catch up with the times, stubborn bits remain. This idea that women are less than men, infused in our laws and educational institutes and structures and economies, is one stubborn cuss. In the country where I live, women have been legally recognized as persons for less than a hundred years. What were we recognized as before that? According to a decision rendered in 1876 by an English court, "Women are persons in matters of pains and penalties but are not persons in matters of rights and privileges." In 1929, women were finally recognized as persons by the highest British court of appeal. But the idea that they aren't still turns up uninvited to every big party in town.

## Mother things

Playtex yellow rubber gloves

Matching Cowardly Lion puppet pot holders

A flattened high school ring run over by a tow truck

Juicy Fruit gum

Kleenex

Macramé plant hangers

Lemon Pledge

Expired library card

Power drill

Small purses that went with outfits

A wedding ring

An engagement ring

A screw-top bottle of white wine kept under the kitchen
    sink

Wooden ladder

Crock-Pot

Learn-to-speak-French cassettes

Sealskin boots

Family photos

Potted geraniums waiting out the winter in the basement

Nescafé instant coffee

Pale-pink nail polish

Coral lipstick

## Mercy gene

When you scramble the word *emergency*, you get *mercy gene*. Maybe that's how the voices came to be, set into action that night by a Mercy Gene. In Janice, perhaps there was some hereditary ability, some innate, biologically predetermined mechanism to provide relief from extreme suffering. Of course, the relief the voices brought was also about suffering, which makes perfect genetic sense when we look at the hot mess of troubled traits she came from. Alcoholics and lopsided varieties of nutcases swing from the branches on all sides of her family tree, and drop like flies at the first sign of heat, as in sensitive and not that hardy.

Her mother blamed her father's side, and her father blamed her mother's side, but whatever, Janice was bred from thoroughbreds that had lost the track and ran about wildly, hurting themselves in pursuits they clearly weren't designed for. If they had been horses, they would have been shot.

Her mother would call this kind of thinking bleak and would always associate it with Janice reading too much, which had the side effect of making her think too much. The first summer of the voices, Janice found that reading kept the angry talkers in her head at bay. She stuffed her brain with the books she could find: *Moby-Dick*, *A Tale* of *Two Cities*, and *Watership Down*, and *Rabbit Run* and everything she could find by Updike, and *The World According to Garp* and everything she could find by Irving, and *Waiting for Godot*, the only thing she could find by Beckett, and *Catcher in the Rye* and everything she could find by Salinger and D.H. Lawrence, and *Dubliners*, though Joyce's *Ulysses* proved to be too much that summer. A librarian recommended *The Tin Drum* by Günter Grass and she read that four times.

Simone de Beauvoir's *The Mandarins* and *The Second Sex* (hidden in the librarian's desk). *That one* went over her head the first time she read it, but some of it landed squarely on her brain the second time around.

With all these words and ideas jostling in her head, she couldn't help herself from bringing big questions to the dinner table. As she passed the mashed potatoes, she would ask, Why seek revenge? Pouring the Thousand Island dressing on her pale iceberg lettuce salad, she'd float, Why does so much love destroy? In between bites of roast beef, she'd serve up variations of the query, What's the point? Her mother was so worried that she took all the books out of Janice's room and in red lipstick wrote on her mirror, "God does not make junk."

Her mother banished her outside and pointed her in the direction of the playground, where the boys hung out, preferring the possibility of a teenage summer fling for her daughter to an apparently toxic exposure to literature. Janice would round the corner and, once out of sight, take the number 112 bus downtown to the library, where she would read all day. A librarian, when told that she couldn't take books home, kept them behind the counter so when Janice returned, she could pick up where she'd left off.

Sometimes, she would pretend that the librarian was her grandmother. She only knew her father's mother as a story, passed down from then to now, with a strange mix of inebriated facts and fictions that changed with whatever haughty mouth told it. One mouth said her father was conceived through an affair. There was an older man, in his thirties, who worked with Edmonton Transit. Her grandmother at the time was a naive young woman, fresh off the farm, exploring the northern Alberta city on her own. The story goes that she fell for the charming streetcar driver, who told tales of the city, as he made his way along his downtown route. In the end, he threw her off track and she smacked into the hard ending of whatever dream she was chasing. A sparrow that flew into the glass, stunned, and left for dead, tossed into the bucket of "one of those kinds of girls." Impregnated by a married man at sixteen.

Another mouth told her father's origin story as a story of rape. And Janice took note of this word *rape* because she'd never heard it before. Janice discovered that rape is one of those words that's both a noun and a verb, a person, place, or thing, and an action. She immediately understood, she had discovered language for what had happened to her, after it had happened.

Now they say that our genes hold the trauma of those who came before us. Maybe genes do hold the facts about our histories, carried within us like locked libraries where the books talk to each other, but we can't hear them.

## Father things

Player's cigarettes

Peppermint Life Savers

White hankies

Business cards

Matchbooks from motels and bars

Black leather pocket-worn wallet

Lethbridge Pilsner beer

The company car, new every year

Hai Karate aftershave

Brown suits

Blue ties

Beard

Alberta vodka

Gold-rimmed glasses

Ray-Ban shades

Eight-track player

A gold-trimmed wristwatch on a worn brown leather strap

Sterling silver shaving kit in a worn brown leather case

Condoms in said shaving kit

Wedding ring

Beer opener key ring

## "Why?" is not a spiritual question

Cells did what they do to make a baby, and I was born in Calgary on an unseasonably snowy day in October. From then on, who can say what was being thrown into the blender or what buttons got pushed and why.

"Why?" is not a spiritual question, someone once told me. I have my suspicions that "How?" isn't either. Look what happened when Stephen Hawking chased that one. Time was just standing still, apparently, and then it exploded and here we all are. I feel like that explosion is still exploding, which of course one theory says it is. But what I mean is that I think I'm closer to the blast's centre than other people might be. Often, I am overcome with the urge to cover my ears and run screaming. It's too loud, it's too fast, and there's nowhere to hide. Still, I try.

Favourite hiding spots: books, my imagination, games, jokes, British crime series on Netflix, lost causes, bouncing a pink rubber ball, bathtubs, philosophical conundrums, work, pretend smoking with Popeye candy cigarettes, in between the lines of good poetry, watching WNBA games, sex, Buster Keaton reruns.

These hiding spots are all a step up from, or at least a sidestep away from, the old hiding spots: the bottom of a glass of tequila, the end of a fist, a padded room, sometimes in a hotel and sometimes not.

I don't really know what it's all about, but here I am, living life as the offspring of my father and my mother. A few years ago, I saw them both during a crisis that was created in a loud and wordy misunderstanding or what they call marriage.

My mother ended up in the hospital with a heart attack that turned out to be Takotsubo syndrome, sometimes called broken-hearted syndrome. It's hard to imagine a more poetically correct diagnosis.

One critical night, my father and I watched over my mother in her hospital bed, one-winged angels previously wounded in separate hunting accidents, both of us remembering to pass the nursing station wing-side in.

When my mother came to, I kissed her sweaty head. She laughed like a toy monkey running out of battery power. I kissed her sweaty head again.

I heard my father say to the nurses, "They're very close, very close." And that lie cracked the hospital floor open, and even though I looked as though I'd been sitting there all night long, holding my mother's hand, I was falling closer and closer to the centre of the blast. My mother and I aren't close anymore. I left Calgary decades ago with a guy who was nice enough to help me get out of town, but not nice enough to stick around with long term. He wound up giving me some bruises, a beautiful baby, a fractured sense of self, a wedding ring I wore for eighteen months, and, when he hit me on the side of the head with a frying pan, the most domestic reason possible to get out of a particularly hellish kitchen. To be fair, I never told him about the voices or how I got them. Sometimes all I could do was rant and rave to keep the voices from leaking out. Maybe if our roles had been reversed, I'd have hit him too. I know we both came from hurt people, and it's bumper sticker wisdom, but: hurt people hurt people. We didn't have a clue about what love or even friendship was supposed to be. I am grateful that we gave each other the courage to leave behind our relative hurts and hitchhike to Vancouver dressed as the 1988 Calgary Olympic polar bear mascots. He was Hidy and I was Howdy, though he'd insist to this day that it was the other way around.

The plan was to ditch Hidy and Howdy's white cowboy hats and matching blue vests and hopefully get work as rare spirit bears on the coast. They say the best-laid plans of mice and men often go awry. This also applies to fake white polar bears.

Now here I am, living life for myself, and although most of the guilt has been worked out of me or talked out of me or repurposed as ambition, I still sometimes wake at night tethered to an ache that I can't name. In the hospital room that night, I watched my mother fight for life. It wasn't the first time I'd watched my mother do that. It probably wouldn't be my last. I had no words to give her. And so, I sang a lullaby that my mother had sung to me when I was a baby, born in Calgary, on an unseasonably snowy day in October.

## A good idea at the time

The Chinese word for crisis combines the concepts of danger and opportunity. When I learned this, from a friend, I had it tattooed on the soft, hairless inside of my arm, just below the palm on my right wrist. It hurt like hell, but I hoped it would remind me that maybe some meaning would come from all this.

Years later, I came to understand that the tattoo artist who inked my skin wasn't as fluent in the ancient written language of Kenji as I'd hoped. The Chinese characters inked permanently on my skin were not the word *crisis*, but instead something that loosely translates to *some sort of magical power over something that was out to destroy me.* Not bad for a mistake.

## What we the voices gave you

Focus. Nightmares. The ability to listen deeply to others. Perseverance. Mental health disorders. Rage. A stiff need to read. Excuses. Unfathomable combinations of swear words. British peers. Gratitude. Broken relationships. An urgent sense of humour. Alcoholism. The will to live. The desire to die. Lost opportunities. Empathy. Earaches. Tenacity. Low self-esteem. Pride. Atheism. Curiosity. The rusted courage that comes with being odd. An addiction to imagination. A great appreciation for orgasms (they always shut us up for a second or two). A practical sense of absurdity, a sick yet friendly relationship with mortality, self-pity, a Whac-A-Mole game right inside your head. Secrets, self-reliance, loneliness. A constantly increasing capacity for uncomfortable feelings. Possibly dandruff.

# Reasons for involuntary admission

Form 13. Mental Health Act, Section 34, R.S.B.C. 1996, c.288

REASONS FOR INVOLUNTARY ADMISSION
A medical doctor signed a medical certificate for your involuntary admission because the doctor is of the opinion that:

a)  you are a person with a mental disorder that seriously impairs your ability to react appropriately to your environment or associate with other people,
b)  you require psychiatric treatment in or through a designated facility,
c)  you should be in a designated facility to prevent your substantial mental or physical deterioration or to protect yourself or other people, and
d)  you cannot be suitably admitted as a voluntary patient.

The reasons why the medical doctor thinks you should be here are written on the medical certificate. You may have a copy of the medical certificate unless the hospital believes that this information will cause serious harm to you or cause harm to others.

As an involuntary patient, you do not have a choice about staying here. The staff may give you medication or other treatment for your mental disorder even if you do not want to take it.

## Janice things

Expos baseball hat direct from Jarry Park in Montréal

Orange notebook

Dave Keon hockey card

Purple Crown Royal bag filled with marbles

Plastic Colonel Sanders piggy bank

Yellow ten-speed bike with Simplex gears

Most Sportsmanlike Player trophy from softball league

A grey-and-faded-orange cat named Cookie

Snoopy Feeling Groovy black light poster

Dr. Pepper Lip Smacker

Blue Adidas Gazelles

Orange terry towel robe

Matchbook collection from places her dad stays in when
    he's travelling for work

Guy Lafleur poster

Grey hoodie

Books: *Black Beauty, The Hobbit, Freddy and the Space Ship,*
    *Nancy Drew: The Clue of the Leaning Chimney, Winnie-*
    *the-Pooh, A Wrinkle in Time, The Phantom Tollbooth, Miss*
    *Twiggley's Tree*

Gingerbread man stuffy from when she was a baby now
    wearing jeans and a T-shirt her mom made

## Certified

Being certified insane means being kept against your will in a psychiatric facility. You are incarcerated, but inside a hospital. Locked wards, bars on the windows. And no guards, just nurses, but male nurses. Big male nurses. A lot of ex-biker-gang guys get sober and become psychiatric nurses. FYI.

The long and the short of it is this: you are certified to protect yourself from yourself.

And sometimes to protect others from you. You start out being certified for seventy-two hours, and if things still aren't looking good, you are certified for thirty days, and that thirty days can be reviewed and renewed until you are no longer a danger to yourself or others.

At any time during your enforced stay, if you feel you're not crazy anymore, you can make your case to a Mental Health Review Board. Sometimes they'll agree and let you go, and sometimes they'll disagree and make you stay longer.

I never went up against a Mental Health Review Board when I was certified insane because, during those times, I was also experiencing the lowest self-esteem of my life. People thought it was about the stigma, but I blame the paper slippers. It's hard to have any game in paper slippers.

I've always thought that it would be great, though, to be told you were sane again. I mean, even when they let you go from the hospital, they don't certify you sane.

I think there should be some kind of paperwork or at least a rubber stamp across your forehead. Sane. Maybe it only shows up under black light. I'm a little ashamed to say this, but even though it's been years since I was certified insane, I still want that. I want some people on the outside looking in telling me I'm sane again. I believe I'm sane again and I know that's all that should matter, but hear me out.

One of the symptoms of psychiatric illness is thinking you don't have one when really you do. So, I wrote a solo play I perform called *Certified* where I turn the audience into a Mental Health Review Board. A Mental Health Review Board usually consists of three people, two psychiatrists and another mental health professional like one of those Hells Angels nurses I remember so fondly. But, I wanted a wider diversity of people determining my sanity, and I couldn't think of a group more suited to the task than people who still go to live theatre.

I give every audience member three cards when they come into the theatre: a red card, a yellow card, and a green card. I tell them, when all is said and done, they will use those cards to vote on my sanity. I tell them my story and it's funny and sad and then funny again. After fifty minutes, precisely the amount of time you'd have in front of a real Mental Health Review Board, I ask each audience member to hold up a card: red if they think I'm still insane, green if they think I'm sane again, and yellow if they can't quite be certain but suggest I proceed with caution. I tell them not to worry about getting it exactly right. I tell them that psychiatry isn't a precise science. In fact, there are no diagnostic tests to prove or disprove that you have a mental illness. Diagnosis involves what's called highly educated guesses. I ask the audience to relax and have fun. It's just a game. Close doesn't just count in horseshoes and hand grenades, it also counts in psychiatry. I've performed this show about two hundred times now in various cities across Canada. Usually people hold up more green cards than red or yellow cards. There is always at least one red card, held high in the air, every time so far by an older white guy. I try to stay focused on the green cards. It feels good to know most people think I'm sane again, at least according to what I tell them in the show.

A lot of people think I do the show for therapeutic effects. What's true is that every time I do the show, I do get something. It's called money.

## Going down

She didn't really think of it as going crazy. It wasn't as if she felt the sensation of descending into madness—well, maybe a little, but it wasn't all that dramatic. It was more like riding an escalator down floor by floor in a pretty okay department store and, after years, arriving in the basement, where all the cheap shit is kept. Even that's okay for a while. The hot dogs are good. It's when the rats take over… Let's save that story for another time.

# The personal is political until it isn't

Before any official grappling with the constructs of gender and the ridiculous limiting of human potential by the sorting of boys and girls into bins of blue and pink, and previous to any luxurious learning where I bathed in delicious and complicated ideas churned up by academia, like genderqueer, followed by the even bubblier non-binary or gender nonconforming/GNC, or my personal preference right now, agender woman, I was just a kid. A kid interested in how things worked and sports and playing in the dirt and using tools, with an insatiable need to learn about people and the ways of the world. I developed the habit of eating questions for lunch when I was very young.

I was both lucky and unlucky that the term *tomboy* existed. Lucky in that it was an acceptable explanation for how I was. When sourced back to its origins, it means a wild, romping girl who acts like a spirited boy. Unlucky in that I wasn't acting like anything; I was just being me. Most of the time, I was allowed to be myself; it was only when the occasion of public presentations arose that I was dolled up. Yup, that was the language used, as in, "It's time to get dolled up." This always brought a smile to my mother's face. She liked becoming a doll, as well as the increasingly difficult challenge of trying to turn me into one. She'd put me in a pretty dress, which I hated because it meant I wouldn't be allowed to climb trees or run. My hair was combed up and gathered into a UFO-sized bun on the top of my head. It was then lacquered in place with VO5 hairspray that made my eyes sting and gave me a headache. The final touch, a little coral lipstick, just like Mommy's, a faint smudge of rouge, and, after I turned twelve, a sliver of sparkling blue eyeshadow. Makeup for me always invited the question, "Making up for what?"

This happened whenever we went to see our relatives, or the families of my father's business associates. In contrast, my brother's hair was wet down with spit, and a fast washcloth was skimmed across his face. Once he had been seen by whoever we went to see, he was free to go and play. I was tasked with sitting pretty by my mother's side. I would start chewing my cheeks, and found that my mouth filled with a bitter, wooden taste from gnawing on the short end of an invisible stick.

As it turned out, gender roles would be the first prescription I wouldn't fill. Sometimes, I am referred to as a masculine-presenting lesbian, historically known as a soft butch. When this happens, I nod and giggle at the same time. I don't know what I hate more, the label or the nod/giggle combo I always seem to respond to it with. Sometimes I wish everything was simpler, that the rules of the world never went beyond trite sayings like *labels are for jars not for people*. But it's hard to be just a jar. The first thing a person does when they pick up a jar is to look for a label(s). If they don't see any, they start to stare, looking for some clue about what's inside you. For now, I and many others continue to carry an unsatisfied longing to just be, neither man nor woman, regardless of the equipment we were born with, free from the judgments of traits and behaviours as masculine or feminine. I feel best in genderqueer and trans spaces where the experience and expression of gender and all its magnificence is present and palpable.

The trouble with some people is that they think we choose the in-between; that we decide to purposely not fit in, that when we defy their expectations for how we should dress, we're doing it for show, to attract attention, not to honour something we know to be true in the stardust of our bones.

We talk a lot about the expression of gender but not so much about the incredibly individual experience of gender. People who never have to think about this have the privilege of knowing they belong to one side of the binary or the other.

We are in the times we are in. I long to see where this all goes, hopefully into never-ending spectrums of gender difference that include man and woman for folks who find belonging there. Imagine each of us, not just tolerated or accepted, but celebrated. Loved, no matter how anyone identifies or doesn't or if that identity changes. Everyone cherished for who they are in any given moment. In the meantime, and it is a mean time, it's easy to learn someone's new name and/or pronoun. You don't have to understand, you can just give a person what they need. It isn't about you. It's also easy to put this sign up on any bathroom door: All Genders Welcome. I believe we can respectfully share spaces to take care of our common human needs: peeing and pooing and freshening up. We

have to share the rest of the world, where both wonderful and scary things happen, so I think we can share the
can. I'd like to see Gender Reveal parties where balloons
are popped and multicoloured confetti floats down on the
parents to mark the joyous occasion of a new being on
the way and all the possibilities that might bring. I'd like
us to think more about the gift of a new life and less about
what we want to wrap it in.

## If I could recast the voices

*List of Celebrity Candidates (in no particular order, in sets of three)*

Miriam Toews
Max from *Where the Wild Things Are*
adrienne maree brown

Lucy Ellmann
Wanda Sykes
Robin Wall Kimmerer

Marcel the Shell
Eileen Myles
Bob the Drag Queen

Catherine O'Hara
Lena Waithe
Ali Wong

Margaret Cho
Peppermint Patty
Pamela Adlon

Maggie Nelson
Candace Parker
Tig Notaro

Louise Erdrich
Julio Torres
Buster Keaton (think about it)

## Paul's Motor Inn

You can't enter the bar from the lobby. You have to walk around to the back of the building and heave open a large metal door. There are red terry cloth covers, elasticized around the bottom, that pop on and off small round tables. The chairs are faded black pleather, puckered and peeling, two per table and set facing the stage. The ashtrays are hard clear glass, with four grooved rest stops for cigarettes, as if anyone ever put one down. The beer comes in pitchers that are plastic, but the mugs are glass and small, half-pints so you can feel you're drinking less while at the same time getting more beer for your money. The only things on the menu are French fries and chicken fingers with plum sauce. The rug—maybe-orange, once-brown, thrown-up pumpkin pie—is too dirty to show a pattern anymore. It looked that way when her father stopped there as a travelling salesman and when Jan did stand-up there, twenty years later.

### 1970

He sits in the bar at the back of Paul's Motor Inn at a small round table facing the stage. He pours from a pitcher of beer. He fills both mugs. He always sets out two, as though he's there with someone else. Someone who just went to the can or maybe to pick up a couple of whiskey shots or maybe some pickled eggs or a bag or two of Old Dutch Rip-L chips. At first, he does his paperwork. He is somebody, obviously, in his white shirt, blue striped tie, and matching brushed silver cufflinks. He jots down details about clients he doesn't want to forget. Birthday, favourite restaurant, wife's name, number of children, hometown, dog? God? He'll transfer these scribblings onto white card stock in capital block letters and then put them into his Rolodex of business acquaintances. He sends Christmas cards to each of them, maybe four hundred, every year. Those with a gold star sticker on the top right corner, twenty-five or so, also receive the yearly family update.

He types the Christmas newsletter himself, made up of vacation reports (holidays where nothing ever went wrong and the weather was always beautiful) and family accomplishments. These were always puckered-up exaggerations he made up about his children by blowing up little inflatable facts he overheard his wife say on the phone. Some kid playing goalie becomes most shutouts ever in the peewee league. Some kid writing poems in her notebooks becomes youngest published writer ever in the *Reader's Digest*. Some kid singing in a junior high school musical production becomes singing professionally at Theatre Calgary. His wife, who volunteered for Meals on Wheels, had always won an award that year for her selfless giving. They are plausible lies, a little outside the ordinary, something people could still see happening without squinting too hard. None of that, or anything else about them, made it onto a Rolodex card. It's odd for them to read about the person their father imagined them to be. It's like reading about yourself as a character in a work of fiction.

When the strippers start, he puts the notes he's making back into a manila file, labelled with whatever town he's in that day selling boxes to people who need them. Lethbridge, Prince George, Quesnel, Trail, Kelowna, Kamloops, Mill Bay, and, on that night, Victoria.

He gets drunk enough to steel his nerves and tries to charm a stripper back to his motel room. Maybe it worked, maybe it didn't.

Either way, he'd pass out for three or four hours of sleep. Alcohol is self-medicating, but so is fucking a stranger, right up until the spasm of coming when the weight of shame lands on his chest like a bad bloated angel, reminding him that he is a failing family man.

The angel then wrapped her thick, feathered wings around his head, providing the only mercy any alcoholic ever needs, a blackout. He will forget everything he's done —and in a drunk's logic that means it never happened. Who can say, though? Maybe he had other reasons for keeping condoms in his shaving kit.

## 1990

Jan has just travelled down from Prince George, where she did a stand-up gig at the Overdrive. On the roof of the club there was a Plymouth Duster, post-crash, with a banner draped across it that read *Get Smashed at The Overdrive*, as if drinking and driving is the point up there. Tonight, she's at Paul's Motor Inn. Didn't her dad give her matches from this place? It's a Wednesday, which is usually Great Strippers of the North night, but they've decided to try comedy for the first time. Jan is headlining and follows Mr. Smut, a misogynistic, racist, homophobic funny guy who is slaying the crowd. They love him. His final bit is all about why an inflatable doll is better than a real live woman. "Their mouth's only for putting in, nothing comes out. And those plastic chicks are there for you twenty-eight days a month." Apparently, he was only counting February. "And if something rubs you the wrong way, you can just throw her out and get a new one." When he's done, Mr. Smut introduces her: "All the way from Vancouver, she says she's a chick, but I mean, come on, please welcome Dan Jerbyshire."

Jan walks through the crowd, noticing men on various steps of the evolutionary ladder, stopping just short of the missing link.

But she knows the rule: you've got to do your time to get your money, so she launches right into her routine. "Hey fellas, here it is, the nineties, and there's still so many things you guys can do that we will never be able to do. I mean, you guys can write your name in the snow." Then she pretends to hold a stand-up microphone, approximately where a penis might be, and, as if the carpet was snow, mimes some loops of cursive writing to spell out the name *Thor*. On a roll she continues, "I mean, women can write their names in the snow too. It's just in braille." She proceeds to hop in a line making pretend pee dots that, to the trained touch, would read *Jan*. No one laughs, and from the back of the room a lone wolf howls, "Show us your tits." Jan is out of heckles. She's heard it too many times. A stripper comes up onstage with her and the whole place goes crazy, hooting and hollering because it's the most famous stripper of the North, Eskimo Pie. She whispers in Jan's ear, "It's not your fault, babe. These boys need slow tit, not quick wit." Then Eskimo Pie saves Jan's ass with hers.

Later, Eskimo Pie, whose real name is Shirley, and Jan, who still goes by Jan, get drunk together. They toast to tits and tequila and Lily Tomlin and good sex and bad sex and pinball and silent films. Drunker and sadder, they raise shot glasses to their mothers, sisters, brothers, and, reluctantly, and without saying much, their fathers.

## Smokes

Janice smoked Export "A"s in the four-foot concrete pipes that were part of playgrounds when she was a kid. The pipes were leftovers from sewage systems or waterworks upgrades, it's hard to say. Slap some primary colours over the outside curves and you're good to go. That's what they made playgrounds out of back then: concrete and asphalt and metal. Kids weren't supposed to be soft. Scraped knees, goose eggs, broken bones, and shattered teeth were all included in the price of play.

"At least you have a playground," her father sang sadly when she made the mistake of wishing out loud about a playground made of mattresses and piles of feathers. Her mother, as she applied peroxide to a cut elbow, inhaled a little shriek of horror about how unhygienic and disease-ridden that idea was.

The Export "A" was her first cigarette, but it wouldn't be her last. The final exhale would be decades away. Smoking would come back to her in fits and starts, an irresistible bad lover that instantly made her feel light-headed, sexy, and sure, and then left her behind—out of breath, tired, and old. But that first cigarette between grade five and grade six with John Paul LaRue was perfect. He called her JD and she called him JP and the cold concrete was perfectly sloped and chilled against their backs on a hot summer day.

They were shaded and hidden from view, and the open-air ends of the pipes minimized the incriminating stench of cigarette in their clothes and hair. The smoke filled their lungs with the polluted sensation of actually being someone.

They stored the pack of smokes and matches in a tiny space between the pipe and the asphalt. They'd come back to find a torched pack and learned to hide the matches separately.

When her mother found a pack of Paul's Motor Inn matches in her pocket once, she lied without thinking. *They make me feel close to Dad*. And that was the end of that.

## Possibly, you were thinking this

Something happened. Something terrible. You don't know what. You are thirteen years old. There is only an ache that can't settle anywhere in your body, it just hovers around you, like a bruise in flight. You only know to keep moving, to keep walking, to create some distance between you and whatever it is that happened. But this ache stays near you like a stray dog wanting you to call it by name. It feels familiar and strange all at the same time. You stop, you have to. You try to take in deeper and deeper breaths as warm blood trickles down the inside of your leg and cramps in your stomach fold you in half. Your brain is full and fast and you can't grab hold of anything that makes sense; words scramble and images are arranged like grotesque collages made by bad artists on speed. You throw up, your stomach trying to empty your head. There is a sound, a single pop, like a gun going off somewhere far behind you. It is a loud dot, the period at the end of a sentence you will never rewrite.

## From Janice's orange notebook, 1975

I am sanity. I live inside a bomb shelter and never say a word. I am relaxed. I read books. I eat well-rounded meals of leafy greens and Kraft Dinner. At night I leave the shelter to walk the quiet of the earth. I walk six miles in a circle with my dog, Logic. I smile at the sleeping people, and they sense me in their dreams. I do not drink coffee, only water from an underground glacial stream. I have a small orange notebook. I write one hundred words a day. This has been today's one hundred words.

### Known triggers (3)

Greasy pianos
Grain dust
French men in Japanese suits
All-day jawbreakers
Bird skeletons
Certain charms on charm bracelets
Chipped cartoon-themed salt and pepper shakers
Broken see-saw
Nice people on the psych ward
Cigarette butts in puddles
These two words together: *animal husbandry*
Lists that end

## Resist

*The consciousness that the patient (person) has of his (her/ their) illness is, strictly speaking, original.*

—Michel Foucault, *Madness and Civilization:*
*A History of Insanity in the Age of Reason*, 1965
(previously published as *Madness: The Invention of an Idea*, 1954)

Don't pick it up. The line, the thread, the unravelling, the thin twine of spider spit. The spider is fucked up on caffeine and thinks thinks thinks it's spinning its web, but it's more like, listen, wheels wheels wheels spinning inside her body head. Resist the caw of the crows, the frogs storming the footbridge, the long and low call of an ex-lover begging you to drop by, a sickening baying, like a moose shot but not yet dead. Resist the Lego raining down that builds itself into a fortress. Your hands feel and smell like licorice babies; don't fucking eat your hands. Here comes some angry focaccia protesting the coming of spring, when people eat less bread. As for the problem with the Wich in sandwich, don't get us started. A placard drives by: *Buses are just limousines full of strangers you haven't met yet.* Some fucked-up fucker wrote that, got paid money for that. Talk about a mind-altered spider spinning a lopsided web. Order another espresso and feel at once spider and fly. Webinars are so fucking ridiculous. Resist the black mould in the wall seeping toward you, a drunken blob high on the prospect of slowly killing everybody in here. Starfucks Starfucks Starfucks. That rings a bell. A ring a ring a ding dong bell. You thought you gave up coffee? Fuck. It's just coffee. Resist the message "run for your life" veined out in the cracks of the linoleum, it's for the poodle half-asleep at the feet of that cowardly manchild that lives in the building next to yours, the one made of Lego, the building and the manchild. Resist making meaning of all this, hear, feel, it's fractured. It's churning brain butter babies with guns.

A lot of perfectly good dinner is going down the drain right now. All right all right all right. Focus. You're caught out, you need to get back to the horn of plenty. Fat red fish gyrate inside lonesome bobby socks. Haiku? Not quite. Fuck you. Michel Foccacia was right about madness being an individual experience. Stigma Fried would have a field day with this. Outstanding in his field making sense of the nonsensical. Stigma Fraud later on, so much later on. I left my heart in Sam Frank's Disco. Bad jokes are bad. The black mood is a crow. Roadkill. Listen, listen, resist the marble ball of under-determined cheese freaks plaster fuck job of horror wink round flabby Madagascar yellow fuck. You do not hit and you do not have a freak out. That mother is talking to you not that little gnome that looks so much like her, also made of flesh-coloured Lego. You don't hit and you don't freak out. We're going to get really angry in a moment. Stop right now. You can't. You can't. There was just too much going on today and we can't explain it to you but it needs to stop. Little Lego gnome breaking down in Starfucks. Climb the walls. Take the vent, Spidey boy, take the vent. We're right behind you.

## Hero's journey

Life as is: Janice is twelve. She is a tomboy. She's playing road hockey with her brother and his friends, pretending to be Dave Keon.

Inciting incident: She takes a slapshot to the chest, and it hits her right in the nipple. It hurts so much she can't believe it. The swelling never goes down. The other side, as if it's worried about being left behind, swells to approximately the same size.

Increasingly difficult obstacles that seem impossible to get through: these boobs, these curves, this moss that shows up between her legs and under her arms, this one extra hole that she has, that the boys don't.

Climax: An urban/rural exchange. Grade-eighters from the country spent a week in the city, and the city kids went to spend a week in the country. Janice took her increasingly difficult obstacles with her. What choice did she have? One night, behind the grain elevators, the girls were hanging out with some boys from town, slightly older than them. There was a case or two of Lethbridge Pilsner beer. Janice didn't notice the other girls leaving. She was drinking beer and trying to find the white rabbits hidden on the beer bottle label. When suddenly, the boys turned into men.

Denouement: In the morning, she woke up and surprised herself by still being thirteen. She had her first hangover. Her body was bruised and scraped, and her one extra hole was so swollen, it was as if it was trying to close itself up.

The next day, on her way home, the voices in her head showed up. Three of them: two women and one man. They were mean and fought with each other.

Janice had to concentrate so hard to not let what they were saying escape out of her mouth, because she knew, even at thirteen, that would make her look like a crazy lady. She had to concentrate so hard she couldn't think much about what had happened.

It's almost as if the voices showed up to help her. On the bus, she wrote something down in a little orange notebook she kept at the time.

## Advice from a madam

*If you're being run out of town, get in front of the crowd and make it look like a parade.*

—Sally Stanford

Their father was familiar with the feeling of being run out of town. Before he was two, the big broom of circumstance swept him from the arms of his teenaged mother, to the hands of her older sisters, to the doorstep of a sad couple from England who now lived in Ogden, a residential neighbourhood in the southeast quadrant of Calgary. Left in a basket for their consideration, he was like some urban Moses, up the creek without a paddle, a replacement baby for their baby who had died from rubella a few months before. He was the balloon baby, filled with the helium of hope, meant to lift a grieving mother and father out of a deep prairie winter depression by being everything they would ever need. They took him in, but he never felt wanted.

Sometime later, who knows where, their father must have heard the above adage from Sally Stanford, a woman who ran one of San Francisco's more notorious brothels. Maybe he heard it there. Wherever it was, he took the advice to heart. When he started to make mistakes in his married life and his young wife threatened to kick him out, that old run-out-of-town feeling came back to him. Thanks to Sally, he knew exactly what to do. Finding courage in the gauzy ease of some drunken delirium, he grabbed the mace of a Drum Major, likely the steering column from his beloved three-on-the-tree 1957 Chevy.

The family didn't think to question their father's take-charge attitude. Masquerading as a responsible man, he knew how to keep the beat. It was easy for them to believe he was the field commander of their little family band, and not someone who was going to lead them astray. And so, they fell in line.

Their father seemed to pick up charm and cunning at roadside stands where others only knew to buy eggs and fruit. With a more precise strategy than the Pied Piper, he rejected the idea of marching them like rats into a common demise, and led them one by one, into a river, a rain barrel, a vat of wine and—for his least favourite—a mud puddle in the middle of the road.

Now this part is only rumour because none of them were there, but one day the Drum Major stopped in a small town to pick up some new epaulettes for his uniform and was surprised when he turned around to find no one was there. With genuine remorse, he sobered up, retraced his route, and plucked his family out of the waters he had left them in one by one.

None of them had drowned, but they were puckered numb, in a state of suspended animation that members of fucked-up families find themselves in during the absences of the one who fucked them up. He celebrated the heroic rescue of his family by picking up the drink again. One would think, having been led astray and separated once, these people would never march behind the drunken Drum Major again. One would be wrong. Bands are full of instruments that don't sound very good when played alone. His return meant they were all together again making music and someone was in charge. It took them a long time to lay their vuvuzelas down.

# Irony is women's work

*Beauty Pageant Winner Gives Up Crown to Protest Skit
Mocking #MeToo*

   —*New York Times*, July 10, 2018

In a skit, the emcee at the Miss Massachusetts competition lamented the loss of the swimsuit competition in the Miss America Organization to the character of God. She told the character of God that she thought the #MeToo campaign was to blame, and the character of God held up a #MeToo sign and said, "Me too, Amy. Me too." Some people apparently laughed, but Maude Gorman, a.k.a. Miss Plymouth County, resigned from the pageant. Competing in the Miss America Organization pageant was a dream come true for Gorman. But the #MeToo joke crossed the line.

At the Miss World pageant in 2015, when she was twenty-one, Maude Gorman won first place in the "Beauty with a Purpose" presentation for a three-minute speech in which she spoke candidly about her experience with sexual violence. She had been raped at thirteen.

"I think society blames victims," she told the *Boston Globe* at the time. "I'm trying to remove that blame. My goal is to be that light at the end of the tunnel for those who feel stuck in the darkness."

—

Maude Gorman and I landed back on the planet in our own time from our own directions.

Her thirteen and my thirteen were forty-four years apart. She didn't tell anyone for three years; it took me twenty-eight. Both of us were jettisoned from the surety of belonging, no longer able to trust anyone's gravitational pull, in orbit around the earth with nothing to hang on to and no way to communicate in a way that made sense to anybody. Both depressed and suicidal and time-warped in blame. For what? The crime of not running fast enough.

She was at the park. Three girls, three drunken men sure-footed enough to chase her and her friends. She was caught and the apes did the rapes. She finally told her mom, but by then there wasn't enough evidence to pursue anything legal. The damage was done, but remarkably, she recovered enough to be able to parade herself with confidence and grace, winningly, swimmingly, through the gaze of men and women judging her in top-tier beauty contests.

I'm happy to see the telling time being reduced. I'm amazed that Maude Gorman told her story inside a beauty pageant. Every #MeToo moment shared and reshaped is a win, as millions of women tell, finally tell, their stories of sexual abuse. It is a reckoning and heads are rolling and maybe we're chopping too fast. But what's unbelievable, what still can feel unbearable — like, it's-killing-me unbearable — is that it's still happening. Those of us standing on the shore are telling and yelling our Me Toos out over waters full of women still drowning.

## Edwin/Raquel

He lays out the sweaters, chalky pastels like after-dinner mints. He lays them out tenderly under the cover of near darkness, flat babies being put to bed on the backyard picnic table. He is humming, Janice is not sure what, maybe something she's heard in church. She watches from under the laundry porch that butts up against the caragana hedge that separates her yard from his. In this spot, where she goes to hide, he is a movie she sneaks into to watch.

The action moves into the kitchen in his basement apartment next door. Janice can see through his large wood-framed window, propped open on this warm August night with a Mason jar showing off some freshly stewed tomatoes. She has a perfect view of the turquoise oven and pink Formica table, where he lays out the pies, tanned crusts with smirks of cherry or apple peeking through. Her dad says he is light in the loafers. She doesn't know what that means.

On this night, she is crying and trying not to. This results in a series of snorts and forced, gobby swallows, sounds that bring him to the window. He cocks his ear and pushes it forward with his delicate fingers. She covers her mouth with one hand and plugs her nose with the other. He looks right at her and then smiles like the cuts on one of his crusts. He is no longer a movie, he's real. In his new dimension he whispers to her, "Do you like pie?"

He is a stranger and a man, a combo Janice has been warned about taking anything sweet from, but she's not afraid. She makes her way to his back door and waits without question as he vacuums the backyard dirt off her with his hand-held Hoover Dustette. A few minutes later, she is eating pie and ice cream and watching him darn soft grey socks.

This is how her friendship with Edwin begins. It lasts the entire year that her father's away, and her mother's so busy working and keeping the house going she never knows. Her brother finds out and tells her that Edwin is a homo, but she doesn't know what that means either.

Sometimes they talk and sometimes they don't. As things progress, he shows her his knitting and decoupage art and how he can macramé plant hangers. She helps out with a few repairs, tightening washers on taps to stop drips, resetting the stove clock, and once catching and releasing a mouse that had him squealing up on a kitchen chair like a cartoon woman.

She learns that his mother lives upstairs, but they never talk. She learns that the sweaters are his and he wears them when he's alone. He learns that her father is in Toronto, finishing up a contract with a pulp and paper company he sells boxes for. He never tells her that he doubts that story because he's seen her mother sneak out at night to sit on the laundry porch to cry and smoke cigarettes. Sometimes, she pulls the phone receiver out the window, its long cord stretched taut as she talks to someone on the other end, sad words between the static.

He almost always invites Janice in when he sees her under the porch. The only time she knocks on his door, his kitchen blinds are closed, and she needs to see him. There is music, and he answers in a dress and makeup and wearing a blond wig. She doesn't think it's weird.

Somehow, in a way she doesn't have words for yet, it makes sense. All she can think to say is, "Edwin, you're beautiful." He pulls her toward him, their first hug, and then whooshes her inside and closes the door behind her. There are three other women there dressed the same way and dancing under a little mirror ball in Edwin's living room. They are fancier than any women she has ever seen, and they move as if they're made out of Silly Putty, stretching out and in, changing shape, somehow holding together.

Edwin says, "This is Evie and Missy and Sophie. For tonight, I'm Raquel. Who would you like to be?"

Without hesitation, she says, "Peter."

## Fuck piss shit

Garble fuck shit piss kill yourself you useless piece of shit listen and learn garble garble garble we should go what the fuck this meeting is fucked the ism I think therefore I'm spam election results temporary insanity squirrels need to go Ivory Coast stop the train heh did you see the game fuck piss shit what a waste of space ice cream headaches remember the forgetting hot house tomatoes broken fucking heart meeting meeting called to order now while the little fuckers listen to music. Yes now. Fuck shit piss. Take a breather asshole #1. I don't breathe you motherfucker meeting meeting come on you fucks now

We're done here

What the fuck? It's boring Preach

Harder and harder to fuck her up

Isn't she a they?

That's just wrong

Harder and harder to fuck they up

Them

Fuck this noise Marching orders Time to fucking go

Where?

When?

Stupid questions

Fuck off

Exactly

Job's not done till she's done
They're done
She she she
Gone soft you fucker
One last push?
Fuck yah
Miss being drunk More than the meds?
Fuck yah.
Prescription Drugs are Play-Doh
Booze is S and M
Fuck yah
Can we get them drunk again?
Push down on those bones there
With what?
The sound of your voice motherfucker
Headache
Headphones coming out
End Meeting
Later
Fuck off
Garble garble me me me me ma. You sorry piece of shit. Hate you. Hate is the rule garbanzo bean misanthrope halitosis fucking dead meat fried on the grill. That one there looking at you like that fucking hates you. Bonkers fucking piece of shit. Ice-cold beer. Die die die. Blah blah blah fuck piss shit losing it man no way you can't even try you sorry piece of shit. You don't belong here, make room for someone else you fuck. Done. You are done. Fucking die you loser you fucking fucking loser.

—

Copy and
Paste
Copy and
Paste
Copy and
Paste
24-7
Copy and Paste

## Heartbreak is to be expected

JD believes now more than ever that this little message strung together from five little words should be repeated to all of us early and often. *Heartbreak is to be expected* should be printed on bumper stickers and T-shirts and mugs, sung to babies as a lullaby, strung across classroom walls, hell, taught as a core subject. Instead of STEM, THEMS: Technology, He*art*break, English, Math, Science. (*Kindly note the word* art *inside the word* heart.) *Heartbreak is to be expected*, sky-written in the blue above all our parades and sporting events, written inside every fortune cookie we eat, graffitied on the sides of bridges, chalked by children on the sidewalks. As it is, most of us smash up against this hard and unforgiving truth like a drunk who wraps their car around a tree, comes to, and can only say, "Where the fuck did that come from?" Heartbreak is to be expected and it will really hurt. It's like this: JD broke their leg once in 106 places after wiping out on a motorcycle. In the ambulance, they howled like a shot dog. After experiencing heartbreak, they referred to the motorcycle accident as their *little biking boo-boo*.

## The online gang

I didn't know what I was doing or where any of it was going to go. I couldn't imagine living with the voices, and I couldn't imagine staying alive on all those pills. Who put the ills in pills?

I found an online support group: Voice Hearers of Britain. I got three e-pals who, like me, live with voices: Schizo Susie, Cray Cray Craig, and One Chip Short. I sign into the chat room as Shit-House Rat. They advise. I take notes.

*All right, the voices, treat them like the bullies they are, ask them to leave, negotiate breaks, you know, I need to focus for an hour, then you can have five loud minutes, listen to lots of music. Drink lots of water, take your vitamins, sleep eight regular hours, exercise, eat all the right foods, no additives, preservatives, colours, no sugar, caffeine, alcohol, or drugs. No smoking. Pause when agitated or doubtful, stay in today. Write. Write, write, write. Avoid toxic people and conversations. Avoid avoiding. Participate. Pray. Meditate. Don't talk too much about poo or pee or sex. Know your limits. Avoid getting overstimulated, try new activities, make friends, keep your world small, but not too small. Be on the lookout for distorted thinking. Trust your gut, learn to follow your own instincts. Be positive, be cautious, but take emotional risks. Work, but not too much. Stay present. Don't futurize. Don't pasteurize. Learn to love your own particular beautiful mind. Get out of the house.*

## Here's one the voices don't want you to forget

Years later, when your Tilt-A-Whirl is just a whirl, you see a man head into the Bow River, determined, sure in his stride, a man with a beard. You think to yourself, maybe it's Jesus. Jesus of Calgary. You think you're funny. The sun shimmered off the water, beatifying his face, and you saw clearly. It's not Jesus. It's God. God, your father. He stops as the icy glacial mountain water hits his knees, perhaps numbing his resolve? To do what? God your father stands fast, in a river greener than envy. What's he thinking about? Has it all caught up to him? What's his all? Is he standing in his own cold river of regret, hoping his heart will finally freeze? Maybe he just can't take it anymore? What's his it? God your father stands there, not moving, like a rock. Is he waiting to be worn down and carried away? You wonder if he's worried about ruining his shoes in the river. And it is that thought that makes its way through all your unanswered questions and propels you into the Bow. As we the voices discuss the possibility that perhaps you will drown with him, you grab God your father's arm and wade him out of the water and onto the black asphalt bike path that ribbons the river.

God your father yells, "Get your fucking hands off me." And you laugh because you have never thought of it that way before, but, as a lesbian, your hands do do most of the fucking.

Fucking hands. Except when the dildos come out, and then—*Fuck*, you think, *I'm thinking about dildos as I help God my father out of the river*. Actually, we gave you that thought. We think we're funny too.

Cyclists buzz past you like frightened flies as God your father continues to swear and struggle, his shit too rank for any of them to even think about stopping to help. God your father stops yelling. He looks at you briefly and suspiciously, like he might know you.

And then, perhaps deciding he doesn't know you, perhaps deciding he does, he flips you the bird and walks away. Remember? You were thinking, what are the odds? That you would be in Calgary for work, walking by the Bow River in the same place and at the same time as God your father was walking into it, maybe trying to drown his sorrows once and for all. Does this constitute a miracle? Can anybody do the miracle math? We drew your attention back to the river. Remember? We suggested you focus your eyes through the sunshine glinting off the crests of the fast-running current. There it was, for all to see. Under the surface, a six-pack of Lethbridge Pilsner beer cans, somehow caught on the grey, rounded rocks on the bottom of the river. It likely fell off a rubber dinghy full of grown-ups, drinking illegally and meandering down the Bow on a lazy summer Sunday. God your father wasn't contemplating the end of his life at all. Of course not, he's immortal, everlasting, living the eternal life. God your father would never contemplate ending it all, he was just out fishing for a free, cold beer.

## Grace

This was the way it was. Any time Jan would move forward into any kind of light, to bask in any kind of positive attention, she would implode: a kernel of corn that couldn't take the heat popped and was promptly eaten. The only movie she was ever in was bad in so many ways. (*Co-Dependence for Lovers*? No, it was *Devotion*. Ha.) She played a stand-up comic dealing with success and sexuality. She was reviewed well. The *Chicago Tribune* compared her to Bette Davis in *All About Eve*, and ironically, because it was 1994, the *LA Times* called her a gay Ellen DeGeneres.

Her response? To disappear into beer, to play Russian roulette with tequila (ta kill ya). She drank away any connections, any future work, any integrity, any anything that might have made her of use to others. She came to with a three-year-old perched on her knee, calling her Mama.

She drove the child to her parents' house and asked them to take care of her while she got over what she thought was a deep depression. She neglected to tell them that the depression was sponsored by Sleeman's Cream Ale and Jose Cuervo Gold.

In her heart of hearts, her mind of minds, her pant of pants, she knew she needed to get sober. But getting off the booze cruise would mean disembarking permanently into the land of voices, and she wasn't ready for that kind of commitment. Alcohol could reduce the voices to a whisper. Quiet, but there all along, the voices amused themselves, taking notes like a dutiful pool of stenographers, typing through the blackouts of a drunkard's private little shame war. They knew they'd have material for years and waited patiently for the day they could bomb Jan with regret for all the amazingly stupid decisions she was making. In the end, it was not the remorse of all the ridiculous one-night lie-downs (standing was out of the question) Jan put herself out for, but the tiny voice of the little blue-eyed one that grew her sense of worth just enough to make her quit drinking. She would call her kid every day, and every day that little person would say, *I love you, Mama*. It amazed Jan. That little voice brought together all the scattered, infinitesimal bits of wonder she had left and gathered them into a ball of strength, iron filings to a magnetic force. And in the mysterious way these things go, a small maternal instinct wound up making her want to live for the little voice at the end of the line.

Jan had absolutely no idea how she was going to be a grown-up, let alone a mama, but returning her empties and donating her beer cozies seemed like steps in the right directions. She had been drinking since she was thirteen, on and off, until the switch broke, and then it was party on, all the time. Thirty-three, she told herself, was a good year to quit—not life, like Alexander the Great or John Belushi—just liquor. How hard could it be?

The first night without alcohol, she went into delirium tremens, the DTs, initials you trade in for any sense of whole words when you suddenly give up the drink. She had no idea what was happening. The smell of her sweet and pungent sweat made her think her apartment was made of rotting oranges. Salvador Dali was suddenly redecorating, melding chairs into clocks and streaming liquid couches out the window to become sofas in the sky. (Magritte took over here.) Traffic passing by outside sounded like wind, and more than once she thought her building was being sucked up into a tornado and carried away. How very Dorothy of her.

The voices grew louder, of course, filling up any silent gaps they could find. At first, giddy with being heard at full volume again, the voices tossed random words to each other, playing a little game of word disassociation they'd always loved. Dog fuchsia neon Bible caravan hula hoop catastrophic disaster disproportionate No Exit Jean-Paul Sartre camp campy little-known fact jelly beans botanist mimosa yellow submarine fool's gold Salman Rushdie tertiary zoo X-rays corn dogs—you get the drift.

And then the bats came, out of a box of Mallomars deserted under her bed. They flew into the room, hundreds of them. The screeches and the smell of their guano had Jan sitting up but unable to flee. In the flap of terror, one bat came near her face and hovered. That bat smiled, bemused and tranquil, and that bat said, clear as a bell, "I am Grace, dare to follow." For the next two days, the bats swarmed, and Jan survived by looking for Grace. She found her a few more times, enough to keep going, and on the third day Jan rose again and followed Grace the bat out the door to a twelve-step meeting that shall remain anonymous.

## What men built

We help you make up lists in your head of what men built: fire and all that followed, weapons and all that followed, the wheel and all that followed, time and all that followed, the Bible and all that followed, money and all that followed, superiority and all that followed, psychiatry and all that followed, laws, politics, language and all that followed, Western thought and all that followed, fear and all that followed, the porn industry and all that followed, etc., etc., etc. Thinking about these things feels big and indescribable. Living inside all of it, all of this concocted cockery, built by man, all of this form and function, deeply troubles you, doesn't work for you, too bad so sad. It makes you feel stupid that you can't trace all the tendrils of patriarchy that have grown up around you, holding you, choking you, bringing you down to one spot where it wants you to stay.

You feel deep shame that the only way you seem to be able to think about it is less literary and more comic book. Patriarchy as a menace, Bow River green with envy, a weed that tells itself it's a flower, an egomaniac with low self-esteem. A ruthless non-native species, sweet-smelling cover-ups strangling anything in their way. *Not fair, Not fair, Not fair* you hear the football stadium full of fans chanting. What about penicillin and electricity and democracy (please, is there a true democracy anywhere?) and X-rays and cheese? Good point, you do love cheese. But still you think, where exactly are they going with all this? Why is ambition a good thing? So little room at the top, another one of their ideas. Yes, yes, make the top pointy so that only one man can reach it at a time and once there is easily knocked off.

You watch a woman weaving through traffic, coming down from something, a deflated balloon after the party, horns honking. A man behind her on the sidewalk yells, "Hit her. It's cheaper to bury her."

You can't help yourself. You want to know who said it. You turn around to see an old white man, with white hair and a white beard, another fallen God still making proclamations from on high (in his case, 5′7″ at best). You want to tell him what a prick he is, how complicit he is in where she is. Based on the time of day and her clothing, this blur of a woman is likely making her way through life in the sexual servicing of men. But the Green Menace of patriarchy is there. It shoots up through a crack in the sidewalk and quickly wraps around your legs and chest and throat before stuffing its foliage into your mouth. The Green Menace believes it's doing its job, protecting you. If you spoke to this little God, he might yell at you, come at you, hurt you.

We spend the rest of the day repeating your fearful thoughts back to you. You go to sleep feeling like a fraudulent feminist. You failed again. You basically left that other woman for dead.

## The uncollected works of a lesser-known Canadian playwright

1987–2000

Tarzana Jane
KC and the Mope Monster
Maharani and the Maple Leaf
Be thee walrus or Yam, I love what I am
How to Rate a Bull's Libido
Labour Unions: The Brotherhood of Mothers
Under the Big Top: Surviving Divorce for Clowns
Joke You
Freaky Jane Fine
Bearded Circus Ladies
The Opposite of Everything Is True
Modern Woman's Guide to Female Impersonation
The Cleaners
Gloom

2001–2007

*No words written*

2008–2022

The Audition of the Embarrassed Woman
West Coast Spectacular
Funny in the Head
All In
Stood
Turkey in the Woods
Certified
Karajokee
Will You Be My Safe Space?

## The telling

For some reason that I can't recall, at thirteen I made the decision not to tell anyone about what had happened. What was I thinking?

Probably that I was in some way to blame. Somehow, I should have known better. I was drinking beer. I wasn't paying attention. I let down my "Lady Beware" guard.

That may have been the name of a film they showed us in grade eight about all the places women shouldn't go alone. If you were alone, the man narrating the film taught us how to hold keys between our fingers, in case. They never really showed us what the "in case" was—the movie just got all shadowy, and the music changed. I know for sure they never showed a grain elevator or teenaged boys. It hadn't even crossed my mind to hold my keys like that. I thought I was just hanging out. I thought I was just one of the guys. I forgot about my one extra hole, but they didn't.

When I finally told someone about the rapes and the voices, I was forty-one. Thirteen to forty-one. I'd waited twenty-eight years. And who did I tell? A psychiatrist. They ask a lot of questions and I had fallen into the psychiatric system because, and I didn't know this then, I had been trying to quit drinking. I went cold turkey. I just stopped. I had unknowingly gone into alcoholic psychosis. *Starfucks. Starfucks. Starfucks.*

There I was, and the doctors over the years had the opportunity to find all these things that were wrong with me that I'd always suspected were there. What's true is that when I was diagnosed with mental disorders, the first thing I felt was relief. My brain was really broken. It had all been too much: being raped, living with voices in my head, becoming an alcoholic, being queer and gender nonconforming, and somehow winding up a single mother.

It's one of the side effects of alcohol that they don't tell you about. If you drink enough, men can start to look like lesbians.

## Why Peter?

Peter is the patron saint of fishermen. Janice thinks of herself as a fisherman. She has her reasons: 1) The way she called the pikes to the boat last summer. 2) The way she learned to catch and release goldeye with her dad on the Red Deer River. 3) The way she waited for hours for that goldeye swollen with eggs to finally swim away, and somewhere during all of that, her dad came back with a sandwich for her and said, "Look at you, Saint Peter."

She is explaining all this to Edwin as they sit at his kitchen table, making devilled eggs for his mother. She is responsible for the shake of paprika dust on the top. She has learned that even though Edwin and his mother don't talk, he makes a lot of food for her. Tonight is her bridge night, and in a few minutes they will walk up the stairs that lead out of his basement suite to the main floor, knock on the door, and hand Edwin's mother three plates: one with devilled eggs, one with little sandwiches that Janice calls gnomewiches and he calls canapés, and one with balls of scooped-out fruit on a stick that he calls melon kebabs. His mother will take the plates one at a time, and when she returns for the last one, she'll nod once to her and once to him and close the door. The first time Janice helped him do this, it made her cry. He passed her Kleenex from a floral-print box and said, "There's all kinds of love, all kinds."

For now, they're finishing up the finger foods, another one of his hilarious ways of saying things, and she is telling him why she picked the name Peter. She was hoping it could be her Confirmation name. As a grade sixer in Catholic school, it's time for her to be confirmed in the Church. Confirmation is the last of the three sacraments of initiation in the Catholic Church. The other two are Baptism and Holy Communion.

You don't have any say at all in either of those, but at least with Confirmation you get to pick the name of a saint to add, unofficially, to your string of names. In her case, Janice Marie Derbyshire would unofficially become — as in not for legal purposes — Janice Marie Peter Derbyshire. You were instructed to pick a saint you admire, with attributes you aspire to. She read everything she could find on the other saints and made what she thought was the humble choice of Peter. She made her Confirmation name presentation to the whole class, as everyone did. They thought she was joking. It hadn't occurred to her that she was limited to only the names of the woman saints. The ten-foot-high HA HA HAs of Charlie Brown fame filled the classroom and camouflaged her red embarrassment as hilarious high-jinxery, as she laughed along.

When the principal, Sister Magdalene, learned she was serious about Peter as her pick, she patiently explained why it wasn't permitted and also suggested Saint Joan if Janice was looking for a little more *masculine* choice. She told Sister Magdalene that she had no interest in leading a war, but fishing had been good to her so far. She left with an absolute no and a string of prayers to say as penance for her misbehaviour in class. She bit her tongue and bled, taking in the tinny taste as a victory for not saying, "Don't you mean my Misterbehaviour?"

After she told Edwin all that, he always called her Sweet Pete, and his other friends called her Peter. After that, she received weekly invites to Edwin's Saturday night dance and do-over parties: fancy invitations, inked in Edwin's fine handwriting, were left in an agreed-upon hidden enclave in the caragana hedge. On Saturday nights, she'd knock on his back door to hear a rousing greeting of "Peter!" She only stayed from seven till nine and was home before her mom returned from her shift at the only Kentucky Fried Chicken dine-in restaurant in the city.

After that, at Edwin's place, everyone brought her ties and suit jackets and men's oxford shoes to be danced a mile in by Sweet Pete.

After that, they even had a faux Confirmation ceremony, where they poured water over her head and fed her bread and made the signs of fey crucifixes in the air. It ended with the presentation of a man-sized signet ring sporting a bold capital P, taped to fit on her index finger and kissed by all the lipsticked lady men.

## Good dog

There it is, the tug of the dog that warns of danger. Get out, trust me, the fire is coming, follow me. Nipping ever so slightly at JD's ass, the dog smells the smoke that JD, in their limited capacity as a human being, cannot. JD needs proof. They hate to run before they have to. The dog begins to panic, weaves figure eights between JD's legs. He huffs out all the alarm he can. For fuck's sake, the dog tries to say, you're the one who lit the match.

JD always forgets that they tend to start the fires. JD is sometimes delusional, inside their own private pyrotechnics show. In this way, JD has burnt down jobs, relationships, friendships, opportunities. It's as if they prefer chaos to the status quo and need blistering heat to feel alive. It happens so quickly, this infernal, destructive rage of theirs. The dog tries to warn them, but come on, who listens to a dog?

This time, JD sees it. The flames leap from their mouth, the person they care about feels the air thicken, tries to talk some sense into them. Fails. Leaves. JD stands fast, the heat of their own anger smokes them, chars them from the inside out, spontaneously combusts them into a pile of ashes that only the dog can recognize. How this dog manages to reconstitute JD has never been fully witnessed. There is a lot of sniffing and howling at the moon, sometimes days of digging, the clacking together of bones, more howling, deep dreamless sleep, static on the radio, and then JD finds their form again and enters the world, a facsimile of their former self.

This is JD's imagining of an emotional support dog. They have read that such a thing exists. They also know that they could never afford a real dog. So they pretend. They have just enough mime training to feel the weight of a golden Lab leaning against their legs. JD calls the dog Paws, a phonetic reminder to pause. In this way they get a little help from a make-believe furry friend, some unbelievably loyal canine vigilance when their own vigilance fails.

Sometimes, it works. Things get tense; JD's not sure what JD's feeling. They say to themselves, *The dog needs a walk*, and head out to stride around the block. Sometimes, they talk out loud to the dog. On the worst of days, you can see them throw a stick, retrieve it, and throw it again. Under it all, mumbled and under the breath, a chorus of *good boy, good boy, good boy*.

## It's a Kacey

When Jan found out she was pregnant, the first person she told was her mother. As soon as Jan got out of the doctor's office, she found a phone booth, and when her mother answered, Jan said, "Hello, Gramma." This surprised Jan. What did it do to her mother? The next person Jan phoned was her boyfriend, the other half of the baby-making equation. She said, "I have something to tell you. I'm having a baby with or without you, you can decide."

Jan was sure that she didn't want to talk about the baby as a she or a he. Maybe she was just trying to manage expectations. The first thing people often ask when they find out you're pregnant is, "Do you want a boy or a girl?" Jan doesn't remember ever being asked by a doctor or an ultrasound technician if she wanted to know the sex of the baby. She doesn't think they did that back then. Jan did endure old wives' methods, like swinging a wedding ring on a piece of twine over her belly. The direction of how it spun revealed that Jan was going to have a boy. The boy theory was backed up by how she carried her pregnancy, like a little basketball in front of her. If you saw her from the back, you wouldn't even know she was pregnant. This meant boy. Jan didn't want whatever was growing inside her to think she preferred a boy or a girl, so she started to call the baby Buddy. *Hi Buddy*. Jan pitched names that seemed to offer non-typical masculine or feminine traits: Casey, meaning brave and courageous; Oliver, as a bring-er of peace. These were agreed upon, and before going into labour, she instructed the boyfriend—who in some wickedly potent spell of conformity cast upon both of them had become the husband—to just say the baby's name, not the gender. Here's Casey or here's Oliver.

And he did. When the baby came out all black-haired and blue-eyed, the father of the baby said, "It's a Kacey." (He had agreed to the name but wanted a more feminine spelling. Jan agreed, but only because the word *ace* was in the middle. Jan liked that.)

So, the story about how Jan got pregnant, told earlier as the joke about how, if you drink enough, men can start to look like lesbians, is a lie. Let's be clear. Men *can* look like certain kinds of lesbians, with or without alcohol, but that's not how she got pregnant.

Her body, when she still shot through the world straight as an error, made a decision and convinced her brain. Her body was persuasive. The decision to have a baby was the clearest decision Jan never made. She told her mom that it was going to happen. On a visit to the mountains of Kananaskis, where they sometimes went for Thanksgiving, Jan and her mom walked through an alpine meadow already brown from the evening frosts, and Jan said, "I'm going to have a baby." Jan's mom may have asked, "Are you sure that's a good idea?" But it might have been the meadow that asked, lying there all majestic, just waiting around for

the snow, humming under the mountain air, *To everything /
Turn, turn, turn / there is a season*. Who can say?

It was a terrible idea. At the time, Jan worked as a stand-
up and a comic improviser, travelling a lot and making
just enough to live on. She shared an apartment with her
ambitious boyfriend, who was trying to break into film in
Vancouver by working as a production assistant guarding
parking spots and picking up cigarette butts. Somehow, his
unhappiness combined with Jan's need to loudly express
her opinions roared them up into terrible fights every three
or four months that included too many moments of WWF
to ever end fairly. He was bigger, and Jan ended up with
bruises down her back and goose eggs laid on her head that
would never turn to gold.

Jan's part in all that was that she stayed. The thing is,
she loved him. She had always been attracted to angry, stray
eccentrics who don't quite pass for normal, and the hitting
seemed at the time to be something about him that she was
failing to understand.

Illogically and irrevocably, Jan went off the pill, and by
the end of that same October she was pregnant. She knew
before any doctor told her. She was doing a sketch comedy
gig up in Whistler, and suddenly beer tasted like vinegar
and cigarettes like exhaust from the tailpipe of a diesel bus.
She put down her glass of beer and ground out her smoke
and didn't pick them up again until after she'd had the baby.

Both of them had been raised by Catholic parents and
although there were no tense meetings of the families to
make a wedding happen, no shotguns aimed at anyone,
and no money to be cut off from, there was an expectation

that they would get married. And they did. Jan had never abandoned herself more completely. Some brides get left standing at the altar; she left herself before she walked down the aisle.

It happened on a February evening, in candlelight. The misfits took the light from candles their parents were holding to light a candle they stood beside for the ceremony. The flowers were orchids. A bouquet for her, a boutonniere for him. Jan's hair was up and sprayed into place. He had a fresh haircut. She had her makeup done. He coated his lips with Cherry ChapStick. She rented an ivory vintage wedding dress. He borrowed a tux. Jan ate blueberry pancakes and shot hoops at the YMCA with her best woman on the morning of the wedding. He drank vodka with his best man right before.

Minutes before the wedding was to begin, when Jan was standing in the vestibule at the back of the church with her mom and her best woman, her mom said, "You don't have to go through with this." It was snowing and a little cold back there and Jan laughed and felt close to her mother. And then she heard the flute music she'd asked her aunt the nun to play, a hymn of her choice that she could walk down the aisle to. Was it "Ode to Joy"? No one seems to remember.

It's hard not to wonder what it would have been like if Jan had said to her mom, "Thank you for saying that, let's get outta here." The three of them would have taken her dad's blue-and-white Dodge Diplomat. Like Thelma and Louise and Thelma's mother, but heading to a much happier ending. They would have called the church from the airport and asked the minister to tell everybody to go to the hall and eat all that great food Jan's grandmother had made. "Eat, drink, and be merry," Thelma's mother would have chirped through the phone. "Celebrate a mistake not made." Thelma and Louise and Thelma's mother would have flown to Greece, to walk and talk and lie topless in the sun. And KC would have been born there, and Thelma would have strapped KC on her back and herded goats and learned how to make cheese and eventually write plays because, after all, Greece is rumoured to be the birthplace of comedy and tragedy. Thelma's mom would take the opportunity to study history and world religions in Athens and come back on the weekends to see the goats and KC. Louise would fix up an old ten-speed bike and ride through Europe. With the change of every season, she would come check in on everyone, sometimes with a lover and sometimes without.

Maybe that's a possibility Jan thought about in the back of the church. More likely her imagination was limited in that moment, suffocating in the container of convention she had agreed to seal her fate in. Also, *Thelma & Louise* didn't play on movie screens till three months after Jan's wedding (google it).

JD still can't believe Jan ever got married. Because it lasted less than two years, JD checks *single* and *not divorced* on census forms. This doesn't feel like a lie. Maybe Jan didn't understand then that happily-ever-after rom-com love runs through her veins like so much bubbly soda from a restaurant offering free refills. Jan was the product of people who were each other's first loves, and who married as teenagers. So was the misfit she stood with at the altar. Jan told Kacey, when she was five and asked, that sometimes you make a mistake and then you have to stop the mistake. Two wrongs knotted together can sometimes be untangled to make two rights. It's the math of love.

## Once you've gone mad, you know the way

It was 3 a.m., and they did ask, but still, going through the Timmy Ho's drive-thru to grab doughnuts and coffees with the paramedics driving me all the way out to the Chilliwack hospital because the psych ward at St. Paul's downtown was stacked to the brim with nutbars and loony tunes was unnecessarily surreal. I mean, come on, there's a time and a place for double-doubles and chocolate glaze, and it's probably not when you've got a suicidal basket case shelved on the gurney in the back. What's true is that they likely couldn't have considered such an early morning snack with any other kind of patient rattling around in the back, and they were sock-monkey tired — five overdoses and one ridiculous car crash already that shift — and I was like a free ride. And also, for the record, I was saying over and over again, "It's okay, it's okay, it's okay." They didn't get that I was saying it to try to keep the voices calm and carry on because I was scared shitless, thinking a person like me doesn't want to end up in a place like Chilliwack, which is more or less exactly what the physiotherapist said to me when she shook me awake to throw the medicine ball around with the other caw caw cawrazies at 6 a.m.: "A girl like you doesn't want to end up in a place like this." Then came breakfast: porridge, Tang, and a prayer led by the hospital chaplain, who went from table to table, insisting that everyone hold hands to better connect with the Saviour. It turned out to be good preparation for my first appointment with the born-again Christian psychiatrist, which also took place in the cafeteria. He wore one of those little ten-week-old-baby-feet anti-abortion pins on the lapel of his serious grey suit and told me a story about a woman he knew who found Jesus and wasn't bipolar anymore. He asked, "Do you want to be bipolar anymore?"

The voices were screaming in my head, and I was wondering how much Jell-O I could get stuck in my throat. For the first time, I felt in more danger inside a hospital than out. Through the windows I could see snow-capped mountains that glowed with an unnatural light, an eerie purple, bouncing from the hundreds of neon crosses topping the spires of churches that seemed, from this view anyway, to outnumber the houses. A gaggle of nurses walked by in company with the physiotherapist, and they all gave me a well-practised stink eye, twitching quickly—north-east-south-west—that I later came to remember was actually them making the sign of the cross with their eyeballs. I didn't give the psychiatrist an answer to his question "Do you want to be bipolar anymore?" mostly because it's hard to wrap your head around clumsy grammar or anything else requiring thought when the voices are screaming. I tried to stay in the here and now by watching the faithful doctor go from table to table, inviting the crazy ones to sit with him at the small bench under the large crucifix, most of them eventually crying and falling to their knees to join him in prayer.

I spent less than ninety-five minutes in the ambulance

getting from Vancouver to Chilliwack, including the pit stop at Timmy Ho's. It would not be delusional to say that even though I'd travelled just over a hundred kilometres, I'd landed in a totally foreign land where Jesus was King. I was a sinner about to be smote or smited or turned into a pillar of salt, eventually ground down by the physiotherapist herself and spread from the back of a pickup truck in the hospital parking lot to melt the never-ending ice that was always tripping up the true believers.

## Punch drunk

Janice's brother taught her to punch one muggy spring night downstairs in the rec room. Upstairs, manhattans were gulped by her father and Fresca from the can was gulped by her mother, and the too-young-to-be-old, married-with-children people pretended, like bored game-show hosts, to be mostly happy. Below them, her brother held a pillow in front of his chest and Janice practised hitting the imagined nose of Christine Happington. Her brother said it was all about seeing the punch through, not stopping short, and she was highly motivated to get it right.

Christine the Wicked had been stealing Janice's Montréal Canadiens toque every recess and throwing it over the chain-link fence that separated the schoolyard from the backyard of one angry and plump Mr. Martini and his Doberman pinscher, Max. The dog was also angry and so fat it looked more like an overstuffed toy. Max had such a terrorizing bark that Janice felt the sensation of blood running down her calves every time she heard it.

Christine would snatch the toque, surrounded by her posse, girls in grade four just beginning to tweak with their new powers of beauty, and lob it over the fence with a dainty but effective arc. Janice would then have to go to Mr. Martini's front door, and walk through his house that smelled of damp biscuits and gin, and retrieve her toque.

Max, obeying his master, would sit and snarl. Once, when Max lunged at her, she scrambled over the fence like a ninja, one of the boys told her later.

Janice had always got along better with boys, who had legs that needed to run and liked to talk more about how things worked than about other people. But even they wouldn't go near the baby-blue-painted talons of Christine Happington.

Janice punched the pillow held by her brother again and again, thinking criminal thoughts she'd picked up from some crime show on TV: *She will pay, she will pay, she will finally pay.*

There was a sharp, acid tang in her mouth, the nervous taste of knowing how much she wanted to hurt someone. Janice had been given the idea by her father when she came in red-faced and crying from school, again. He happened to be home (an odd occurrence) and seemed happy to see her (way past odd and into Strangeville). The world tipped upside down the moment her father asked what was wrong, as if they were in a snow globe together that someone was shaking, little flakes of kindness floating down around them. Or was it ash? Sad ice clinked in the glass as her father said, "You need to clean her clock."

The next day, armed with her father's advice and the new skill acquired from her brother, Janice landed a perfectly executed punch that connected with the small, pert nose of Christine Happington. There was a dull crack, and then blood exploded like liquid fireworks, bright red and beautifully weird. Christine crumpled, her screams fluttered the nuns into action, and even shut up Max the dog. When Janice's mother and father were called in to Mother Superior's office, the father from the snow globe melted and denied it all.

Janice was expelled for a week, but her mother seemed to know that her father had lied about not giving her bad advice. She never said as much, but she took Janice to Science World twice that week and even volunteered for the electromagnetic experiment, placing her hand on the silver ball and letting enough electricity crackle through her to set her hair straight up on end. It was the best laugh a mother could give a ten-year-old tomboy beginning to doubt her own mind.

## Another one of their theories

They are big on this one: you have to love yourself before you can love anyone else. We, the voices, were never going to let that happen. In fact, for the first sixteen years that we were with you, we kept you from even coming close to liking yourself. We delighted in generating and sustaining your self-hatred. Most days involved an endless string of generalized cruelties: you useless piece of shit, what a fuck-ing fuck-up, loser, asshole, pain in the ass—over and over and over again—piss, shit fuck Christ, Jesus fucking Christ, kill yourself now. These brain heckles were supplemented by echoing some of the thoughts you were having about yourself: I'll never amount to anything, I am broken and so fucking beyond repair, I'm a waste of space, a nothing, a fuck-up that no one can love.

Deprecating thoughts are notoriously clichéd because negativity eats creativity like so much cheap lunch. There were, however, a few dog-paddles of happiness that we were unable to drown. The first of these was the ticking of your biological clock. You didn't even hear it, but we did. It led to a drunken night of unprotected sex with an unsuspecting straight shooter, or so you like to tell in the *Reader's Digest* version of a story that actually stretched out over six years, where a boyfriend became a husband and you became a wife. Anyway, somewhere in all that, there was a miraculous yet mundane human moment when sperm barged into egg. And then time, as steady as a metronome, lulled the little blue-eyed one into a calm and measured becoming. And even more miraculous and less mundane was that we couldn't get to the little blue-eyed one. She was completely unaware that we were screaming inside her mother's head.

When she was born, she looked at you with unconditional love, a term both rom-com writers and psychologists make a lot of money from; one sells it and the other one buys it back.

It was a look of love so pure that even we were surprised when you could return the same kind of look to her. We took it as a sign to redouble our efforts. Right there in the delivery room, we turned up the volume to eleven. When you wanted a beer, we knew why. And no one was surprised that your dad brought a couple of cold ones to the hospital with him, just in case you asked.

## Mother Brother

On Mother's Day a few years back, Kacey gave JD a moustache made from human hair that she crafted in a workshop she took. She calls JD Mother Brother, which is fair and right for so many reasons. They did grow up together. JD thinks of parenting as a time when they stood with their hands outstretched and ready at the side of the trampoline, a spotter. JD said to Kacey, "I'm here if you need me and somewhere else if you don't. Just keep trying more and more difficult tricks and if you fall into my hands, I got you."

Make no mistake. JD would have preferred to have got their shit together before having a kid.

JD suspects that nobody ever gets their shit together, and that possibly all parents don't know what they're doing. But because JD couldn't deny that they were getting some big things wrong, maybe they had a kind of humility that other parents don't.

Kacey is an adult now and has her own shit to pick up and put down and never get together. Some of that shit has to do with JD, some of it doesn't. Kacey has already gone through the therapy money JD saved up for her as a child. It was a jar on top of the fridge, labelled *Therapy*. JD would put money into it after they'd had a fight or if they'd handled something badly. When Kacey moved out, JD could only give her $256.45 in coins, but it was something.

## How to get off the bridge

That one time she phoned the suicide helpline and heard Rufus Wainwright singing "Hallelujah" on the other end, all tinny and sincere.

When she saw the brown-edged grocery store carnations someone had tied to a beam with a bungee cord.

When she found the note tucked into the railing: *Despair is not always unreasonable. I am simply no longer seeking reasons to live.*

When she met the old man who'd walked on from the West Vancouver side dressed in a kimono who told her he liked to walk the bridge at 3 a.m. looking for people like her. He said, "Whatever that song from *M\*A\*S\*H* may have claimed, suicide is not painless. You will hit the water at approximately 138 kilometres an hour, smashing your bones in an unnatural crash, unlike the God-geared collision of atoms and stars that you were born in…" She walked away and missed the rest.

—

A seagull speaking in the voice of a dead lover, quoting from a note she'd left behind.

> A *leaf falling seems like a random act. But each leaf, triggered by a sequence of amino acids in DNA, falls when it is ready. When you see that leaf fall, aren't you overwhelmed by the feeling that this leaf knew exactly when to let go?*

Hunger. Specifically, a craving for chicken soup with matzo balls made by Sol in his bagel shop.

## Margot Kidder

One day Jan overhears on the bus that Margot Kidder is coming to town:

Who's Margot Kidder?
You know, Margot Kidder, Lois Lane—Superman's girlfriend.
Really?
Yeah, from the really old *Superman*, like, your dad's *Superman*. He's dead now.
Oh.
And she's bipolar.
She likes to make love to both men and woman in really cold climates?
No, she's crazy, but doesn't take any drugs anymore.
Weird.
Riiiiiight?

Jan goes to hear Margot Kidder give the keynote speech at some orthomolecular psychology conference. Lois Lane speaks: *Bipolar. Bullshit. Nutritional Deficiencies. Mental Illness. Physical Illness. Head not separate from body. Biochemical Imbalance. Not Chemical Imbalance. Too many Drugs. Not enough Vitamins. Minerals. Amino Acids. It's a Physical Fucking Illness.*

Jan experiences her first tickle of hope in 700,432,000 seconds. She imagines Margot flying down the aisle in her perfectly pressed suit, wearing Superman's old blue tights underneath. Margot Kidder scoops her up and flies her out of the hotel, up and over downtown, and lands her in a swish naturopath's clinic on Broadway. In about half the time it would take on transit, and she flew for free. Thank you, Margot Kidder.

Jan quickly discovers she doesn't have the kind of money it takes for the kind of alternative treatment she needs. The government will pay for drugs and hospital stays but not vitamins and minerals. But fear not, Margot Kidder is here. Margot signs a blank cheque to cover everything she'll need. Now that's Super Ma'am!

Jan comes out of her daydream in time to see Margot signing autographs for a long line of orthomolecular psychologists she will never be able to afford. She leaves and goes to the library where all poor people go to learn. She reads what little she can find on alternative treatments for mental illnesses.

Jan discovers that some psychiatric medications can actually cause suicidal ideation. She finds this organization called the Icarus Project, with all this information on what pharmaceuticals can and can't do and how to safely get off as many of them as possible. She feels crazy but begins to slowly wean herself off the meds and takes as many vitamins and minerals as she can afford.

She takes a job at Starbucks. It's the only job she can get. Her resumé has become a bit spotty over the last few years.

*Customer*: Could I get a half-fat, no-foam, extra-hot cappuccino. Tall.

*Jan:* You know, caffeine does not give you energy. It stimulates your nervous system, and that's not energy, that's stress.

*Customer*: Make it a Venti.

*Jan:* Sure.

## Jan things

Nestlé Quik hot chocolate tin that holds the following:

A picture of KC, blue-lipped and smiling, shivering in a
    yellow bathing suit by a lake

Keys to dead Grandma's car on a kilt pin

Apology letter and dried rose from the first boy/man she
    fucked

Mood ring

Dave Keon hockey card

Tickets from Fleetwood Mac concert

A few shredded pieces of divorce papers

Three cheap medallions from half-marathons

Sobriety chips 30, 60, 90 days

A pack of wildflower seeds

Kacey's first baby Adidas

Leather bracelet from Mexico that reads *Jan*

Various rocks collected by Kacey

*Carpe diem* ring from first Queer love

An undeveloped roll of film

Toronto transit token

A postcard from France from a friend a few months before
they died

St. John's Ambulance first aid training card

Orange notebook

Matchbook from Paul's Motor Inn, Victoria, BC

## Snap

Snap. A twig on the forest floor. Snap a chicken neck before the plucking. Snap. A card game. Snap. An alternative to buttons (often found on Western shirts, sometimes called rape shirts in the seventies because they could be ripped open with one grab). Snap goes the human brain. Here one day and gone the next. Snap, Crackle, and Pop. The sound of a breakfast cereal. Nothing to worry about here. Move along, move along.

## I am Canada

I am Canada. In me, I carry the genes of the English and French colonizers of this land. The Plains of Abraham stretch across my belly, continuing to churn. *IBS* in my case stands for Internal Battle Scene. My gut is always where wars of trouble start, where anything unsettled goes to fight, where lines of enemies charge each other with hollering belches and pointy sticks. The land of my stomach is never settled. It's been like this since I was a kid.

I was raised by the English and the French. Although both of them were several generations from their ancestral homelands, my parents were political caricatures who cartooned our house with the pride of nationals who had never set foot in England or France. They were capable of the relative congeniality between Canada's winning and losing conquerors; but my parents never understood that the war had ended and, like fatigued soldiers who forgot what they were doing, fought on.

My mother France fought for freedom and fun and independence. What my father England defended most were the rules. He was raised by British immigrants, a mix of the Isles really, some Irish and Scottish tinges, but he was loyal to rules of Britannia. He travelled for work, but when he was home, it was truly his castle and his rules. Children were to be seen and not heard, adoring and unquestioning; curiosity was left under the porch like a stray dog you hoped could be kept fed without getting caught. Manners were prioritized as indicators of goodness and even sanity, if we can all agree that sanity is abiding by the rules. Conformity was expected and deviation was punished with the withdrawal of affection at best and ass spankings and belt whippings at worst. Everyone beat their children back then. Spare the rod, spoil the child.

I always got in trouble when England ruled. I couldn't manage to leave France behind fast enough and would talk out of turn or be five minutes late to the dinner table or crack a joke at the wrong time. Sometimes, a stern stare would warn me that the flag flying above the house had changed, but sometimes it would provoke a laugh as fast and musical as the French language itself. I would be banished from the room to be dealt with later. This, of course, was where my stomach trouble started.

When my father was gone, the windows were opened to the breeze of Joie de Vivre. Locks were unlocked and people came for bowls of soup, free advice, hand-me-downs, chocolate chip cookies from the freezer, card games, and singalongs. Many of my friends liked my mother more than they did me and would hang around until she insisted on driving them home. There was laughter and spontaneity, and people ate standing up, leaning against kitchen counters, cross-legged on the floor, or on a lawn chair brought in from the garden shed as needed.

In this messy milieu, my mother confessed her thwarted desire for a big French-Canadian family, and first told me about her miscarriages and my miraculous birth. My brother had been born and then me. Between us, she lost four babies early on. She was convinced that they were all little girls, so when I was born a girl, she rejoiced. Unfortunately, *la fille* didn't turn out as she'd hoped and so she glommed on to my girlfriends like bad mascara. In fact, she hosted free makeovers and hairdo jams while I busied myself outside, cleaning out the gutters. She had given me a choice: yardwork or participation in the afternoon salons. She thought I would hate yardwork more than her little offerings of home charm school.

She guessed wrong. I loved being high up on a ladder by myself with leather work gloves on, scooping out the mess of dead leaves and dirt that had accumulated over the fall. I thrilled at hauling up the garden hose to run water through the eavestroughs until they drained free and clear. How could she have known? My brother was also happy standing below, hands clasped tightly on the ladder rungs, watching all the girls get pretty through the kitchen window while I did the chores assigned to him.

To her credit, once my mother France saw that I loved the kind of work normally left to the men of the house, we often did it together. She was a whiz with repairs, and with me as her assistant we fixed washing machines, dishwashers, stiff locks, broken porches and fences, holes in walls, a kitchen radio, a clutch in a Fiat, garage-door openers. We bailed and resealed basements stupidly built on flood plains. Somehow, we found nicknames for each other; she was Fred and I was Joe. We'd put on work jeans and old bleach-stained sweatshirts normally reserved for camping and get the job done.

There was, however, a catch. England could never know. It was one of the secrets in my childhood that I agreed to keep without knowing why I was keeping it. There was a trace of an explanation, the screech of a bomb that had already, in the distance, struck its target. I faintly remember hearing something along the lines of, "Daddy would prefer if his girls didn't do the dirty work." I don't know what my mother called the work of the kitchen cleanup after another Sunday dinner was made, doled out, and devoured by fifteen people, but to me that was the dirtiest work of all.

Fred and Joe wasn't the only secret. In fact, all the Joie de Vivre times when England was away sailing the seven seas were encouraged to be thought of as undercover operations.

If not top secret, then at the very least middle secret — the kind that, if leaked, wouldn't likely lead to war but could make trade negotiations between France and England difficult. It still amazes me, all the rules you go along with as a kid without ever asking why.

Sunday dinners were the only times in my home when I felt the presence of both countries at once. I have clear memories of standing on the border between the kitchen and the living room, unable to choose one side over the other. In the kitchen, all the women of France covertly enjoyed themselves under the guise of cleaning up the mess. They would laugh and tell jokes, impersonating their husbands, often complaining of serious injustice under the purposeful frolic of it all. They also served as each other's lookouts, stealthily checking in on the whereabouts of the men but sure that none of them would set foot in the kitchen until all the work was done.

In the living room, the menfolk of England drank and talked ideas. Well, it was more like they blurted out opinions and didn't really listen to each other. They howled out their thoughts like wolves stuck in their own traps. Even so, I liked to hear what they were thinking about the government and the oil business and money and the NHL. I offered an opinion of my own once or twice, and would get pierced by the tiny-arrowed ideas they had about women, small but sharp enough to make me cry. "Don't worry your pretty little head about all this. You'll be making babies, not money." I squeezed my eyes shut, trying to find words, but only tears came. This would happen often in front of men in the future when I tried to say what I thought and was made fun of. Back then, I was rescued by my mother or an aunt, who would flap back in to refill beer glasses and empty ashtrays.

Then she'd nest me into the kitchen again with a sweet smile and a little whisper, something along the lines of, "Just let the men be."

France gave me my sense of humour, ability to keep secrets (even when keeping them was devastating and destructive), my handy ways, my fear and its best friend, hyper-vigilance, my sometimes hatred of the English, my disdain for domesticity, my quiet, churning opinions that sometimes explode in rage, my attraction to funny, strong, and bordering-on-martyr women, my Montréal Canadiens fanship, my crying as a go-to response to any emotion, my devotion to brie cheese, and my deep and lasting love of maple syrup.

England gave me the low self-esteem of the battle weary, distrust of authority, the deep-seated need to hide happiness, an addiction to needing to be right, a twisted acceptance of violence, smoking, drinking, and other bad habits of the civilized, unwarranted and patchy audacity, and the unfathomable grief of a winner becoming a loser and not being able to admit it.

Together, my parents gave me the embodiment of my first schism, a mind-splitting division between strongly opposed differences in opinions and beliefs. Did they also give me an internal battle between delusion and reality that would later be called a mental illness?

I do not think minds are lost. I think minds are taken when we are young, in wars that aren't even ours.

## Some thinking JD thinks

Between 2000 and 2005, Jan was in and out of psych wards every six months or so. Every time she left the hospital, she felt as if she were walking on carpet-covered sand, sinking down with every step but not quite deep enough that she couldn't move. In downpours that slicked back her hair and dripped off her nose, she walked to the Lions Gate Bridge. The rain melted her like sugar, inviting her to disappear. She was frightened, flattened out in that place between not wanting to live and not wanting to die. After getting out of hospital, she would walk to the bridge almost every night for months.

Hunger was far and away the most common reason for coming off the bridge. Sometimes, looking back, it seems to JD that the brisk middle-of-the-night walk was simply what Jan did to work up an appetite.

JD also wonders if going to the bridge was Jan's way of strengthening her ability to make the right decision. Every time Jan walked away from the railing and back to solid ground, did the voices lose? Was Jan proving to herself that she was really in charge? Despite not being able to fight the voices' commands to go to the bridge in the first place, did Jan have some sense of victory in being able to get off the bridge again and again?

Jan saw and heard many things on the bridge. Real or imagined, it's hard for JD to say.

Madness brought her to the bridge and imagination brought her off the bridge? Too simple. There is such a fine and mysterious line between destruction and the construction of a lie or a reason or a fragment, a figment, a song, a piece of something said in a way that Jan could hear, that kept her from falling.

The police call suicides from bridges jumpers, but that's too strong a word.

It's not an active going into, it's a soft opting out of, a surrender. It's a fall, a falling, less of a statement and more of a question that can't be answered or a thought that can't be completed and so…

For Jan there was a method that never failed to make her stay on planet Earth. In the midst of the voices doing what they do best, repeatedly spouting reasons, horrible reasons, why Jan should no longer exist, a sentence would fight to be heard inside her head: *Your presence will be required at a later date.* JD has no idea if Jan had read it in a book, heard it on a TV show, or maybe made it up herself. It didn't really matter where she got those words, the point is they worked, every single time.

A question that often keeps JD company on their long Hi-Bounce Pinky ball bouncing walks at night is this: If Jan could make up the reasons for staying, could she also, in some devastating and self-hating way, conjure the voices themselves?

## For those of you considering madness

A good mad is hard to find. But if you find one, hold on tight. You will be given wisdom and insight and stimulation, and things might even make sense. I mean, everything might actually make sense for about ten seconds. You will likely forget those ten seconds, but the experience of being in the know, however briefly, will make the rest of your life seem pointless and beige.

Why would anyone toy with all the other shit that goes along with madness for those ten seconds, especially if you're just going to forget? Good question. If you have to ask, you've obviously never been there. If, however, you're nod nod nodding your head in that knowing fashion of yes, yes, I think I've been there but I can't be sure, as you scan these letters from left to right, if you've actually felt a pang of longing for something you can't really remember, so deep in your gut you almost threw up, if you know with great certainty that you shouldn't read any further because you will be licking your lips with the missing of madness before the end of this page…welcome, my friend. Everything's going to be all right. I am here for you. A sentiment you know to be pure bullshit, despite people's best intentions; one is always alone while spiralling down into the fast and nasty thick sand of insanity.

Not only can no one ever be with you on this highly specialized and radically individuated ride; you wouldn't dream of grabbing the hand of your own worst enemy for company. Sure, that ten seconds would be great to share with someone, but do they know how to catch bullets in their teeth, or speak Warbaloobee to the cops, or liquefy in a nanosecond to slip under the door as the woman-hating elephants charge? These are the special skills the mad have honed that they can list on a resumé, if they ever get well enough to have one.

# If you don't tell anyone, it didn't really happen

The problem with not telling anyone about something terrible that happened to you is that, without realizing it, you take the side of the perpetrator(s). You become complicit in the crime. For every moment you don't tell someone about what happened to you, the fuckers not only get away with it, but you begin to doubt that it even happened. Because because because how could you have survived something so terrible? Because because because if you keep thinking about it, without telling anyone, you'll go mad.

So she tries to let the violence fade like red paint. She's left with a blur in the bottom of her head, a pink pond turning alkaline and disappearing. Details lost like odd socks in the dryer. There is no proof, real or imagined. No one will believe her. She has trouble believing herself.

She buries the dangerous hot truth. Now it's a fire travelling underground, down to the roots of everything, igniting random trees out of nowhere, the destructive rage of unhealed trauma. She douses the flames with booze and any dirt she can find and wonders what the fuck is wrong with her. All this damage and destruction to herself and anyone who tries to love her.

—

Twenty-eight years later. She watches the doctor watch her. She tells him what happened. It feels like a lie, like she's saying something she hopes provides the reason, the single, solitary reason that makes sense of how she became so fucked up. He immediately focuses on why she waited so long to tell anyone. There isn't even a nod to the horror of what happened, a flower thrown on the grave. Her singed wires and charcoal memories are hosed down with pharmaceuticals meant to extinguish the flames, but really, really, really, they are only dousing what's already been burnt to the ground. Psychiatry asks what's wrong with her, not what happened to her, which, at that point in time, is just fine by her. She hums "Ring of Fire" while she waits for the doctor to speak again. He is flipping through a big book of psychiatric disorders, looking for her new name.

## Lavender version

The one person Janice thought to tell was Edwin/Raquel. But by the time all that ugly went down, her family had moved away to a bigger house in a better neighbourhood. Fresh paint. Fresh start. It was what her father wanted after he returned. She heard him say it as her parents talked at the kitchen table late one night. Ice cubes bumped up against amber glasses, and whispers wisped up and out the window like so much exhaled smoke from a good long drag on a Player's filter cigarette. She got her own room, a calico kitten, and a pass for ten free movies. The last time he'd gone away for a year and then come back, all she'd got was a kite. This was bad. Janice knew this because she was learning to codify what things meant in her family. Gifts or getting things you'd always wanted meant something had gone wrong and you were being bought off to not ask any questions.

Sure enough, it didn't take long for the bigger house to fill up with bigger problems, bigger voices, bigger points of no return. There were more stairs to tumble down, more chances to fall from grace. More rooms with locks to hide or get trapped in. More windows with thicker drapes to be drawn. The appliances were all new and wouldn't need repairs for years. Her mother took up interior decorating, one room at a time, rotating all the way through the house only to begin redoing the first room again. Janice endured the paint and fabric stores but always preferred when something necessitated a visit to the hardware section of Canadian Tire. Fred and Joe reunited briefly to build a ten-speed bike Janice bought from Consumers Distributing. The bike was purchased with the first profits from her paper route — an ingenious solution for covering up insomnia with ambition, after the voices came and sleep ran away with all her sheep.

One morning, after the papers were rolled and tossed, Janice rode to her old house. The black-and-blue exterior had been covered over in the light browns and off-whites of a stale wedding cake. She got as far as Edwin/Raquel's door before she started crying. Her first instinct was to scuttle underneath her old laundry porch next door, but, when she looked, it was gone. The new owners had torn it down and replaced it with a deck. There was a barbecue and wooden chairs, as if the people who lived there actually sat around outside together with nothing to do but eat burgers and shoot the breeze.

The summer Janice and Edwin/Raquel became friends, she'd hidden under the laundry porch every day for a month. She'd made a deal and wasn't a person who liked to lose. Her mother said if she could go thirty days without crying, she would get a new baseball glove. "If you wanna play like a boy, don't you think you should stop crying like a little girl?" her mother said. That question went straight to her head like fishing line, and tangled up all kinds of other thoughts she was having but couldn't find the words to say.

She never got the baseball glove. She learned to hate herself for how oversensitive and immature she was. When she told Edwin about it, how weak not getting the baseball glove made her feel, he told her that crying was a central part of being human. He said, "We pee, we poo, we cry. Crying is just another way the body has of relieving itself, a biological necessity for girls and boys and men and women and everything in between." After that, they would sometimes go and sit on his brown-and-orange couch, find an old movie (like *Love Story*), eat pie, and cry together.

On the day she rode her bike back to her old neighbourhood and found herself slumped down against Edwin/Raquel's door crying, she knew this could go one of several ways. She could knock on the door and Edwin/Raquel would find her and she could tell him everything that had happened and he would know exactly what to say and do. Or she could leave and not say a thing. Something in her believed if she said it out loud to anyone, that would make it true. She was trained in the keeping of secrets and knew that eventually you forgot why it was a secret, and then, with enough time, you forgot the secret itself.

Let's just say she went away; she didn't say anything. Let's just say she didn't even knock on the door. Or let's just say that Edwin/Raquel heard her crying in his sleep, like a falconer hears a lost bird returning to the gloved hand—in this case, white satin to the elbow, with three mother-of-pearl buttons. He was wearing these, and although it was six thirty in the morning, Edwin/Raquel was impeccably dressed in grey, centre-creased, pleated trousers and a white dress shirt under a lovely lavender cardigan. Inside, raisin pies were just coming out of the oven, and Janice was offered, and enjoyed immensely, her first cup of coffee.

Let's just say Peter and Edwin/Raquel just sat there and cried. They cried the kind of crying where there's hardly any sound and water just falls out of your eyes and keeps falling as if inside your head is a hidden lake that contributes to a major tributary heading to the ocean, and all that water is falling down the cliff of your face, heading for the great Continental Divide.

Which way will it go? And let's just say that they cried so much that the pies floated away and the coffee mugs floated away and then, buoyed up by all that salty water, they floated away too, but only as far as the living room.

Let's just say the other lady men showed up with a borrowed sump pump and a disco ball and they danced as the apartment dried out. And let's just say that somewhere in the tang of salt and perfume, of man sweat and lady tears, of all that floats between this is this and that is that, Sweet Pete stood and told the basement Queens what had happened behind the abandoned grain elevator.

And after all was said about all that was done, let's just say that, without speaking, candles were solemnly lit, honouring something that was gone and would never be back. Let's just say furniture and lamps and cupboards were shrouded in clean white cloth. Let's just say the lady men dressed themselves in all their finery, while Sweet Pete sat in an armchair, covered in an afghan Edwin had made, the colour of grain-elevator green. Let's just say that after the

Queens were as queenly as queeny Queens can be, they tailor-made a dark-blue three-piece suit for Sweet Pete. They cut and stitched, and day turned back into night, and the shoemaker's elves and some other little fairies of lesser fairy-tale fame came to help with the making of the suit.

Let's just say Sweet Pete bathed in sangria while all the work was done, and everyone was drinking from the tub. When Sweet Pete emerged, she was pink and she understood that she would have to learn to be okay with that. Let's just say they dressed her in her perfectly fitting blue suit with a white shirt and a blue tie and a bonus gift from the shoemaker's elves who, it turns out, were there to make shoes after all. The shoes fit her to a T, and she understood this was the way she would walk through the world: pink in men's shoes.

Let's just say the Queens picked her up and carried her like someone dead, out of the house and down the street, porch lights dominoing on as they passed. The parade of the in-betweens sashayed and marched on, and instead of jokes and sneers, neighbours came out holding lit candles, honouring their own gendered losses, and joined the parade. Men wearing matching earrings and summer shifts pulled on quickly over their heads, women wearing leather work gloves and cowboy belts and buckles, everyone understanding that old ideas about men and women needed to die. They all walked as far as the park at the end of the avenue. John Paul LaRue was there with a fresh pack of Export "A"s. Sweet Pete, raised from the dead, was put back on solid ground by the Queens. She looked older and wiser, forever changed but okay and kind of handsome. She smoked in front of everyone, and the voices left, catching a ride on some of the perfect O smoke rings she blew. The pack of Export "A"s was passed around, and everyone smoked as if there was no such thing as what was bad for you or what was good for you.

Somehow, in that moment, they all understood that picking sides might be the root of all our evils.

Let's just say that even though none of the others knew exactly what had happened to Sweet Pete, the Queens knew, and for now, that was enough. The air was electric with possibility and gratitude, like the charge of feeling lucky you get when you watch a big storm pass over you. There was a lightness that didn't suit the time of day, like alpenglow when the sun has already set and the tops of mountains appear luminescent. The hue was hope, the park was overflowing, and strangers found strangers and told each other a secret they held about their particular pain of being a man or being a woman. And then the waterfall tears came again, but this time, everyone cried in pinks and blues and the water flowed together and everything around them turned lavender, known for bringing tranquility but also the colour of kingship, excess, and feminine influence. Boom. 'Nuff said. The calming lavender flowed around the world and changed everything. It was the end of misogyny, homophobia, transphobia, and all sexual assault and rape.

Let's just say that's what happened.

## This is the plan

JD will convince the voices that it's time for them to go. It won't happen overnight. The persuading will go on for years, in gaps when JD is alone and can talk out loud to them. In the shower, as JD makes morning coffee, in the car, or on their bike, walking down the street pretending to be on the phone, in bathroom cubicles (tricky), on a late-night bus (also tricky and will likely make the drivers nervous), and maybe sometimes as a little twisted lullaby JD will sing to them as the voices fall asleep.

Here are the essentials of what they'll tell the voices: "Thank you for everything you've taught me. Thank you for everything you've tried to protect me from. Thank you thank you thank you. But really, I'm fine now and I just wanted you all to know that if you want to, you're free to go." Basically, JD will talk nice. They won't yell or scream or beg them to go. They'll appeal directly to the voices' sense of purpose.

"You must be bored. You must be frustrated. I know you know that you just can't get to me the way you used to. I'm sorry it's not much fun for you anymore. I imagine you feel unimportant and not useful. I know that's a shitty feeling. So go, why don't you just go? It would be really great for you to go. I will miss you. I don't know what I'll do. But it's what's best for you. You should go. You should go now. Please."

JD will think of their mother every time they talk this way. Their mother taught that, sometimes, talking nice to fucked-up bastards is the only way to survive. Unfortunately, it doesn't make anyone want to leave. It won't make the voices leave either. Why would anyone leave someone so nice?

## Apples and oranges

My parents tell this story from a decade ago about being in the backyard peeling apples all day to freeze up a winter's supply of applesauce, and how they had a good time with each other, talking about nothing big, and my dad says, "Funny how we never find the time to talk." When they came back inside, the song they woke up to on their honeymoon, "What a Difference a Day Makes," was playing on the radio and so they also took the time to dance. My parents have always waved happy stories in front of my eyes like shiny gold watches on chains, a form of hypnosis, the trance of denial. Not that they didn't have some good times, but the bad times were cut from the movie, like they never happened.

For me, scenes smash up against each other. Geriatrics-making-applesauce love in the autumn smash cuts to summer horror: accusations of dementia, letters delivered to each other's doctors begging for tests to prove the other's rapid decline. It's always been a wild show, a couple of real live wires exposed and dangerous, like lightning in a prairie sky, best watched from as far away as possible. They sometimes insist that I am making the bad stories up. I am the crazy one. I feel better when I stop asking for any of it to make sense.

What if, instead of standing for the singing of national anthems at the start of sports events, we linked arms and cried? Sobbing for all we've lost, for all the loss to come, for all we will never understand. What if every day was a kind of personal Remembrance Day, and we stood for a moment in the closest thing we can get to silence? Because there, in the distance, are the sirens of emergency circling us all. I can imagine the ambulances getting closer and closer for my parents, who, as so many of the self-help books say, "did the best with what they had."

My father has been lost for a long time. Alcoholics are suicides we watch happen in slow motion. Our grief is scattered year after year like breadcrumbs on a trail we know will never lead us home.

But my mother? I've likely been running away from the idea of losing my mom since I was five, when she was sick in the hospital. Sick of what? In deep pain, she knit sweaters to pass the time. My brother and I stood one windy Sunday in the parking lot to let her see how well the sweaters fit.

It has been like this since then, me waving up to her, trapped behind a window, both of us trying to look happy with no way of getting to each other. And my father, is he up there with her? No. He is standing some distance off, smoking a Player's cigarette. When we drive home, it will be dark and we will sit in the car before going in. He will pop a peppermint Life Saver in his mouth and chew it. Sparks will fly from his mouth. For some reason, peppermint Life Savers did that back then. I have never wanted to look up the science behind it. I prefer to think of it as the only magic my father had to give. After the sparks trick, my father hit the road to sell whatever he was selling those days.

My grandma was inside, waiting for us, caring for us while my mom was in the hospital, while she healed from something they whispered about as a tipped uterus, which I heard as a tipped octopus. I fell into certain kinds of deep-sea nightmares for years because of this little misunderstanding. When I learned the truth, I couldn't bear to think about it. I actually preferred to think of the octopus story, and picked it up from the old-ideas trash pile and told it to myself again and again.

A lot of people talk about how important it is to forgive your parents before they die. There is nothing to forgive. There is only the grief to carry, the decision to keep waving as the window they stand behind fogs up and suddenly, what will seem like suddenly, they disappear.

Or you can find the stairs and take them up to see them whenever you can. I realize this. I am a grown-ass person; I don't have to stand in the parking lot anymore.

A few years ago, I was in my parents' backyard and my mom was showing off the gladiolas and the clematis and the roses still blooming into early September. I stopped to smell a rose, and she saw me and smiled. Maybe it really is this simple, maybe this is all the sweetness life can give, a little clichéd moment like this. To focus on the scent of a rose—not to block out all the dying and the decay, but to choose in the middle of it all to sniff out a tiny bit of amazement, which your mother happens to see.

In the garage are piles of boxes and bins that she has been keeping for me for decades. I have never owned a house and the storage space that comes with it. She wanted me to go through these. She's clearing out what she can in case they need to move into assisted care in a few years. I have purposely stayed light, leaving the hard evidence of life behind as I've moved from city to city over the years. She has secretly been accumulating, mostly from my daughter's childhood. We opened the first bin, and I saw my daughter's favourite bucket hat, red with white flowers; she wore it all the time when she was five and six. There was a small piece of paper pinned to it that read: *Kacey's hat*. With a closer look, I saw strands of hair wrapped around the pin, the auburn colour of then. I started to cry. There were twenty boxes to go. I said, can we do this next time? And my mom said sure.

At the airport later, I wished we hadn't let all the phone booths disappear. I wished we'd converted them to cry booths for all the adult children fresh from visiting their parents behind the glass, trying to look like grown-ups and waiting for their flights home. Cry, cry, cry, it is the only thing to do. It is the correct response, to cry.

# After fifteen years of talking to the voices nicely

JD feels as though they're getting somewhere, because sometimes they catch the voices having little meetings amongst themselves to talk about the possibilities of leaving. They gather in a little hollow where the back of JD's head meets their neck. JD listens in, even though they get a blazing and sadly specific ache in their eyeballs, as if someone's jabbing in those little corn-on-the-cob holders that look exactly like corn on the cob. JD slowly figures out that the voices want to leave, but they don't know exactly where they came from or where they might end up going. They are afraid. They don't have a plan. JD will make one up for them.

## Dear Margot Kidder,

You saved my life and now you've taken your own. I am deeply unsure about how this makes me feel. One fist shakes angrily in the air; the other clumsily punches my own eye, a bully looking for tears.

I saw your passionate, spit-flying speech that backed mental illness up against a wall and had it falling apart like a papier-mâché man in the rain. I saw the way your hair flew with the wind kicked up from your large-gesturing hands. I saw your generous, floodlight smile. You were not an example of the subdued and formerly crazy; you were a slightly reined-in wild woman who refused to give up all the fruit in the basket just because a bad apple had been found.

You were preaching to the converted, orthomolecular psychologists and supplement salesmen, who sat rapt in hard-backed chairs under the high, decorative ceiling of the then-named Hotel Vancouver. You pontificated on the successful use of megadoses of vitamins and minerals and amino acids in the treatment of so-called mental disorders.

You didn't deny the symptoms you suffered from, the extremes of mood and the distorted thinking that at its height saw you running through the streets of Los Angeles like a maniac. You were simply reminding everyone that the head is connected to the neck is connected to the body, and maybe these so-called chemical problems in the brain are in fact biochemical imbalances and maybe, just maybe, what we put into our bodies has some effect on our minds. You said you'd found a good mix of your eccentric self and relative stability using alternative methods of treatment. You, Margot Kidder, gave me hope that maybe life could be worth living again.

Inspired by you and under the care of a forward-thinking GP and a naturopath, I managed to reduce and eventually eliminate all my psychiatric medicines. I got sober, with the help of too many people to name, and learned how to be mindful and meditate and all kinds of other hippie shit that has given me a pretty good day-to-day.

What I will never be able to give up is the hyper-vigilance that comes with hearing voices and being what some call bipolar. This requires self-determination of what behaviours are too high or too low, what thinking is off track and heading toward distortion, and how good or bad my capacity for uncomfortable feelings might be on any given day. It can be done. But I know in my heart of hearts and my mind of minds that letting your guard down is what likely caught you, Margot Kidder.

I don't blame you. It's exhausting trying to make sure you're okay all the time while trying to live a full life. It's hard to know who you can talk to when it gets bad. If you tell mental health professionals what you're really dealing with, the treatments they'll likely prescribe will zombie out everything about you. I get it, Margot Kidder. You start to isolate and before you know it you're inviting Death to dinner, and he's asked those two old friends, Alcohol and Drugs, to tag along. And you sit around, stuffing each other with the richness of loneliness, indulging in decadent despair, and then Doom crashes the party and the exit door beckons. It happens so fucking fast. I get it. Many of us do.

One thing I know is that you were likely in mental anguish beyond what most people will ever know. I hear a lot about people who don't take their medication and how everyone seems so shocked that anyone would do that. I don't hear as much about those who've actually been on psychiatric medication and know what the medications take from them. You, Margot Kidder, were one little celebrity voice trying to tell the world that psychiatric drugs aren't magic; they don't actually work that well for some of us, and many of the side effects are debilitating.

Psychiatry is good at temporarily saving a life, but not at helping you go on with wanting to live one.

What's also true is that vitamins and minerals and amino acids aren't enough on their own. Maybe you got caught, Margot, between tides of conflicting theory and you just grew tired of the swim.

I feel crazy saying this, Margot, but my voices have told me more than once: all suicides are assisted suicides. As a so-called civilized culture, we do seem trigger-happy quick to write off those who suffer from so-called mental illness. The best we have to offer are mind-numbing drugs that don't just tame the wild, they shoot the horse and think it's just playing nice as it lies down in the barn.

You hated the stigma of mental illness and hoped we'd find new words for it. What could we call it, Margot? How could we treat it with the best knowledge from all the fields of expertise?

Thank you for saving my life, Margot Kidder. I'm sorry I couldn't return the favour. I feel so sad. I have to go and cry now. It's the next right thing to do. Then I will get back to being vigilant.

## Recently known glimmers 1

*\*Glimmers are the opposite of triggers. They don't get much press, like good news. A glimmer is defined as a small moment that sparks joy or peace that cues our nervous system to feel calm or safe or happy.*

Discovering the concept of glimmers as defined by Wikipedia when I googled *what's the opposite of a trigger?*

Thinking about what kind of theatre or stand-up show would have a glimmer warning

Riding my bike down a hill and closing my eyes for a few seconds

Toddlers running and not falling

Eating cheese pizza hiding under an awning in the rain

How KC makes me laugh with her impersonation of Alanis Morissette

Snow globes from places that don't snow

A long, deep drag on a Popeye candy cigarette

Colossal squids

That two women married to each other both play on the
   Chicago Suns WNBA team and won the championship
   in 2021

The older lady, with a Philippines flag hanging from the
   rear-view mirror, carefully driving by, hands at ten
   o'clock and two o'clock. She has kept her four-door
   Corolla looking so good. She bet on herself when she
   bought it in the nineties.

The leaves that fell as they poured the cement and
   embedded themselves just near the surface of the
   sidewalk on 6th Avenue, like the stars in the Hollywood
   sidewalks. In Vancouver, maybe the Big Celebrities are
   trees.

Bouncing a Hi-Bounce Pinky ball

The movie *Inside Out*

The book *The Disordered Cosmos: A Journey into Dark
   Matter, Spacetime, and Dreams Deferred*, by Chanda
   Prescod-Weinstein

Swimming in a lake at night in the summer

My mom's paintings, especially *Psycho Cat*

## Out of the house in 2005

I was down from thirty-six to twenty pills a day. I was feeling a little better. I'd joined a writers' group with Ivan Coyote, I'd called up some old friends like Mac and Misha. I volunteered at a seniors' centre teaching improvisation for shy people and started to play road hockey with a bunch of Queerdos behind Britannia High School in East Vancouver.

After the five years I'd had, I thought, if this is as good as it gets, this is good. And then something miraculous happened at road hockey. A woman starts to talk to me. She wears a faded yellow shirt with a *B* on it, blue cord cut-offs, and pink Adidas shell tops. She's beautifully athletic and she scores a lot. She is completely out of my league. Turns out this woman is a mechanical engineer. I feed off this woman's rationality, while this woman feeds off my whimsy. We do things, together. We walk and see shows and make love and the woman makes me eggs. There are longer gaps between my spells of wanting to die. I avoid the hospital, but I'm pretty emotional and cry a lot. I tell my new girlfriend it's because I'm the sensitive artist type. My new girlfriend finds that endearing because she's a fucking engineer. When we've been together awhile, I offer her the only truth I have at the time: "I'm an alcoholic who tries not to drink anymore and I'm on some psychiatric medications." The new girlfriend stays. I stay. We learn to dance together, which is harder than you might think for two women because, who the fuck is leading? I feel myself falling back into life, falling back into love, I wean myself off a few more pills, but then the voices come back. I can't tell my new girlfriend about that. As a general rule, women who love women have a lot of room and acceptance for eccentricities and traumatic pasts, addiction and the lighter-weight mental illnesses (depression, anxiety, ADHD), but hearing voices—who wouldn't draw the line?

I am so down and out that all my new girlfriend can think to do is spoil me. For our second Christmas together, my girlfriend gives me snowshoes. Really beautiful, blue, expensive snowshoes. I break down. "I don't want snowshoes. Margot Kidder. Want naturopath. Megadoses. Allergy tests. Neurotransmitter tests. Takes money. Need help. Snowshoes nice, sanity better."

My girlfriend takes the snowshoes back to Mountain Equipment Co-op and funds my treatment until I am well enough to fund it myself. I continue to detox from my pharmaceuticals; it takes half the time that you were on them, years in some cases. I get a therapist and start to learn about the long-term effects of trauma on the brain and the body. I get megadoses of vitamins, minerals, and amino acids. I am relieved of the desire to die, but the voices grow louder and louder. One night, in desperation, I take myself back to the psych ward. Before I see a doctor, I decide to call Schizoid Susie, my e-pal from the Voice Hearers of Britain, from a pay phone in the hospital hallway.

*"Darling, please. Stop with the sobbing! Listen to me, darling, darling, you're absolutely right. If you go back on the*

*medications you were on, the voices will go away, but so will so much more, you know this, sweetie love love. Mine have never gone away, darling, good days, bad days.*

"*I get triggered, darling, and they get loud. You can avoid some triggers, sweetie love, love, but if you've had trauma in your past, you will always get surprisingly triggered, pushed from the now into the then, barely able to keep your head above water in a flood of great big feelings that have very little to do with what's actually going on in the here and now. Oh no, sweetie love, love, there is no avoiding the flood. (Singing) 'Just keep swimming, swimming, swimming.' Too soon for Dory, darling? Listen to me, sweetie love, love, you can deal.*

"*You've already had all this time learning how to increase your capacity for dreadfully, uncomfortable, feelings. Temporary feelings. Remember what Schizoid Susie taught you to say when those big tsunamis of emotions come?*"

And I remember.

"*This is an old feeling. I don't deserve to feel this much fear, anger, anxiety, abandonment, shame. I am here. It is now. This will pass. The wave is not the water. The wave is not the water.*"

Susie says, "*Say that to yourself, darling, a thousand times a day if you have to, sweetie sweetie, and you can live your life.*"

I hang up the phone and leave the psych ward for what I hope will be the last time.

## Already I'm so lonesome I could cry

JD has a plan. They hear it first in their bones, the ones at the back of the head near the neck, where the voices like to meet. JD has convinced themselves that the only way for them to be free of the voices is to send the voices to someone else who has experienced what they did. JD starts to imagine what they'll do with all that room in their head, with all that quiet. Will it be quiet? They feel amazed by the possibilities. JD also feels weird, like a person who keeps checking the lottery numbers even when the machine blinks YOU'RE A WINNER. This is a genius plan.

They will all go back to where they first found Janice. They will go to the exact spot. They will wait for the sound of a siren in the distance. The siren will get closer and closer. When the ambulance passes by, the voices will fly out of JD's head, little cartoon demons hitching a ride. They will travel with the sirens until they find another thirteen-year-old girl/woman lying dishevelled and confused, with a brain cracked open just enough to let them in. It won't be hard for them to find another girl/woman to fuck up completely. It's still happening every day.

Wait. This is not a winning ticket. This is not a genius plan. JD wouldn't wish these debilitating motherfuckers on their own worst enemy. JD has mostly tamed them. It has taken years. They can't bear the thought that someone else would have to start at the beginning with these cruel loudmouths. There is a collective sigh of relief between JD's ears, like the sudden warmth of a chinook wind. And then, as if the voices feel it's important to let JD know they're still here, they turn up the volume: Fuck fucking piss garble garble fuck head fuck, fuckers, you useless piece of shit. Party on.

## Goodbye, Doctor

Even after the hospitalizations stopped, I still saw a psychiatrist once a month because I had a mental health team; it was part of my treatment plan. For two years, I'd been taking the prescriptions he gave me and not filling them. I lived in fear that he would find out I was completely off my medications. He could brand me as non-compliant and put me back in the hospital. He had noticed positive changes with me: less suicidal, more friends, a relationship, writing again, working again. I decided to give him the whole story. I wanted to move him from one part of his brain to another, to shock him out of something he was so sure of into something he was not so sure of. I wanted him to help me imagine a better world where we would start an organization that saw naturopaths, psychiatrists, and trauma therapists working together. We would call it the *Fund a Mental* Foundation. When I'd finished telling him my amazing story, he said, "I've watched your progress. I knew it was too good to be true. There can be only one conclusion: you must not have been mentally ill in the first place."

I could feel the wind ripping off my mental labels as I waved goodbye to the doctor and started to dance-walk home.

I felt…so fucking freeeeee…freeeeeeaked out.

I had been a psychiatric in/out, in/out, in/out, in/out, in/out, in/out, in/out, in/out-patient for five years. The various diagnoses were always there, waiting for me. At any time, when I couldn't handle things, I could just say, *I live with a serious mental illness and too much is being asked of me.* And with that, I could stop having to be so hyper-vigilant about my thoughts and feelings. I could stop being so careful and cautious and responsible for all my behaviours. Now what? I was so afraid. I felt the big black bird of self-doubt circling. I wanted to go back inside. But I didn't.


Years since I've been certified: 19
Years off excessive pharmaceuticals: 16
Years of active harm reduction from alcohol & drugs: 22.5
Years without a doughnut: 0


From that day forward, February 14, 2006, till today, I just keep figuring out what works for me. I'm making it all up as I go. The worst thing that all the medications took from me was my imagination. It's impossible to imagine not having an imagination until you have an imagination again. Turns out that's what I need the most to get me through.

# I am a figment of Miriam Toews's imagination

A few years ago, I was in Calgary standing beside my car, parked in the spot beside my parents' garage. In the house, my mom is terribly sick and my dad is trying to deal with all of it by drinking beer like he's twenty again. Who can blame him? Everything in my oversensitive, over-emotional self knows that what's going on inside my parents' house is way too much for me to handle. So, I make a decision. I think about Miriam Toews, the Canadian novelist who has written many amazing books, though I'm a huge fan of *All My Puny Sorrows* and *Swing Low*. She does this thing where she writes with exquisite tenderness about mental illness. She writes about all the really horrific things that happened to people in her family but also about everything they were inside the lives they lived. Then she seems to make up stuff around it that helps her make sense of it all. She fictions her way through the facts. So I decide, standing in my parents' driveway, to imagine myself as a figment of Miriam Toews's imagination. She's definitely whose figment I should be. I feel real, but I'm not, I'm completely made up. That's how good Miriam Toews is.

I walk to my parents' back door and turn the knob. The door shatters into shards of ice. I step over the ice and into a house full of winter. I feel frightened. What if Miriam

Toews doesn't even care what happens to me? I mean, I'm not even family, at best I'm Miriam Toews's imaginary friend. Does she even know yet if this is a comedy or a tragedy? "Same thing," I hear Miriam Toews say, as though she knows what I'm thinking. Oh wait, she *has* heard me thinking; she's thinking it for me.

Miriam Toews is sitting at the kitchen table, drinking beer with my dad. He's completely covered in polar bear fur. Was he always a polar bear? Had I just failed to notice? Miriam Toews wears a T-shirt and cut-offs. Dad says, "She's originally from Manitoba," as if that explains why she doesn't feel the cold. Mom calls to me from the bathroom. I look to Miriam Toews. She flicks her hand out in front of her like, Go, go on.

I find my little mom standing on the toilet, wearing polka-dot pyjamas and lighting match after match. She passes some to me to light. "I'm sorry," she says, "but a husband should never smell a wife's shit." I say, "But Mom, you've been married for over fifty years." She laughs, lights another match, and says, "And this is why."

I walk my mom back to her bed. She is as thin and tired as a hungry winter sparrow. She is asleep before I can say good night. At the kitchen table, polar bear Dad and Miriam Toews are playing caps. My dad is losing. He starts to slide under the table. I reach for him, but he slips through a hole in the ice and lands perfectly on a grass-thatched stool at his tiki-themed bar. In the basement. He puts on his favourite Johnny Cash album, *Ring of Fire*. His polar bear fur turns a lovely shade of amber and then falls off. He sits there naked, drinking rye. When he sees me peering down at him, he closes up the ice-hole hatch.

Miriam Toews cracks open another beer. "When in Alberta," she says. She unpacks a little green typewriter and holds it in place between her knees. She says, "Tell me what happened in the bathroom."

I say, "Don't you know?"

"Out of sight, out of mind," she says.

"I don't remember," I say.

"Make it up."

"Why don't you make it up?" I say. "You made me up."

Miriam Toews looks at me for a long time. I know she chooses words carefully, so I wait. She finishes her beer and finally says, "You're going to have to let go of this whole figment-of-my-imagination thing soon."

"Why? It's not hurting anyone," I say.

"It's delusional."

"I thought you'd appreciate that."

"I do," she says. "I just worry. I tell stories. I can't make this any easier for you."

I say, "Since when did stories make things easier? Have you read your own books?"

Miriam Toews passes the green typewriter over to me and says, "Just get down what happened in the bathroom; you might need it later."

Instead, I type:

*dear miriam toews,*
*i take great comfort in being imagined by you.*

*maybe it's as close as i can get to believing that there's
something out there that gives a shit about me and the
people i love. is that so crazy?*

*signed,*
*you know who*

Miriam Toews smiles the way Mona Lisa would if she
hailed from Winnipeg. She pulls what I've written out of
the typewriter, folds it neatly in thirds and then in half,
and hands it to me. I put it in the back pocket of my jeans.

I still have it. Authentic proof.

The heat from the lava lamps in my parents' tiki-bar
basement and the hot crooning of Johnny Cash starts to
melt the upstairs. Miriam Toews grabs her typewriter and
rides a small iceberg out the front door without so much as
a goodbye or a see you later.

A rush of frigid water pushes me back out into the yard.
I stand in the moonlight in a river up to my knees. The
birdbath and some small shrubs get carried away. I stand
fast. I watch the water level come down inside the house.
Everything returns to its proper place. The furniture drifts
back into the living room, the drapes hang beautifully,
everything shines with a deep, deep clean. My mom walks
into the kitchen. I watch through the window as she peels
and eats a banana. She stares out and over my head at the
stars in the sky. My dad comes upstairs, a little drunk but
soft and smiling. He and my mom dance so slowly that they

look more like two old people just trying to hold each other up. I stand in my parents' backyard, watching the last of the ice age melt away. I feel useless and sad. I wish I was somehow more of what they needed.

I get as far as the car before I don't know what to do. Luckily, Miriam Toews returns and kicks open the passenger-side door with some cowboy boots she won off my dad. "We played some poker," she says.

I say, "I feel like I'm in a barrel about to go over Niagara Falls."

Miriam Toews says, "You're in your car. Put the pedal to the metal and let's get you home to Vancouver."

We drive from Calgary to Canmore, listening to nineties rock.

When I pull in for gas, Miriam Toews goes inside to pick up a pack of Twizzlers. I could drive away and leave Miriam Toews at the Mountain High Esso station. I could make a clear choice to sever reality from delusion. I don't. Miriam Toews gets back in the car. She pulls out a thick yellow pad and starts scribbling. "Somebody's got to get this shit down," she says.

We drive west through the mountains. I talk the entire way. She writes down what I say. As we approach the west coast, the colours around us drain out. The rain comes in steady waves, and grey permeates everything. It feels personal. It's not. It's just November in Vancouver.

Miriam Toews says, "You know you live inside a teardrop, right?"

And I say, "Miriam Toews, write that down!"

## Dear Doctor

Sometimes, I imagine telling a psychiatrist: Here's how I get through tough things these days. I believe I'm a figment of Miriam Toews's imagination. And then I imagine telling him, Look, I'm most certainly a woman. I mean, this was the form I was given, but it's heavy. It's heavy with expectation, it's heavy with meaning, it's heavy with history. And so I kind of fill it up with the lightness of a little boy, you know, like helium made up of all the curiosity and excitement and mischief and exuberance and energy people think of as boy. So, Doctor, if you're going to force me to identify, I am less Woman and more Woboy. And you know, Doctor, I'm never without my Hi-Bounce Pinky ball. I bounce it walking down the street or off walls, it keeps me out of my head, it keeps me joyful. I'm sad every day. So I cry. We pee, we poo, we cry, as Edwin said. I can still get angry quickly, but I'm learning to take smoke breaks. I don't actually smoke anymore. I use Popeye cigarettes. All right, all right, Popeye candy sticks. I inhale deeply, and yes, I've tried it without the candy sticks. I can't do it. Usually after three to six deep drags on my candy-stick cigarette, I can calm the fuck down. I've never felt saner, Doc, if sane is some sort of agreement to just stay with yourself and all your fluctuating moods and tangential thinking and sensitivities. I am still a voice hearer. I hear voices, yes I do. I hear voices, how 'bout you? Mine are a bunch of whiny singsongy naysayers, disgruntled and dissatisfied and hell-bent on my destruction. At times one of them will take on a solo, belting out an abusive aria over and over again on a particularly dark night. My own little choir of doom and gloom. On a good day, the voices are like a radio playing on low in another room. On a bad day, they're louder. I talk to them now. Every day, I tell them, I don't need you anymore, your job is done, you're free to go. Maybe one day, they'll listen. And yes, I have read my files, Doctor, and there seems to be more than enough evidence to suggest that I have some higher highs and some lower lows than some people. But I will never believe that means that I, or anyone like me, should be chemically disabled from living a full and fruitful life, emphasis on fruitful. I think we've been lied to, Doctor. I think we've been told that we can achieve stability in our emotions and security in our lives. But the truth is, we are all on shaky ground that sometimes cracks wide open, and we fall for a while into the pit of unavoidable human despair. And then we're spit out again. Pit and spit and pit and spit and pit and spit. I appreciate some of what you did, Doc. I think psychiatry is good at interrupting minds in crisis but not so good at helping us live well into the long after that follows a crisis.

Then I show him the tattoo on my wrist. I tell him what it was supposed to be, the Chinese word for crisis: danger and opportunity. Psychiatry can treat the danger and I thank him for that, and then I suggest that perhaps they are still overmedicating us away from opportunities.

So I imagine telling a psychiatrist all that, and he looks at me and says, "Well, if what you're doing for you works, it works...for you." He considers the Miriam Toews story payment for our session.

## JD things

Levi's 501s

Small notebook in back pocket

Black Flair pen

Membership card for Ucluelet catch-and-release aquarium

Plastic turkey key chain

Vancity Visa

WNBA basketball hoodie

257 books

142 notebooks

MacBook

Lego Sesame Street

Two typewriters

Toronto Blue Jays vintage jacket

Red-and-white Nike Blazers

Grandmother's old radio

Pictures of family and friends

Bronner's peppermint soap

Old Nestlé's Quik tin

Orange notebook

Grey T-shirts

Matches from Paul's Motor Inn

## Joseph, Estelle, & Inez

JD is trying to give the voices all the attention they really deserve. Turns out delusions don't think of themselves as delusions. After tuning into several of their meetings, JD discovered their concerns about not knowing where they came from or where they would go next. Without a past, it's hard to know what direction points toward the future. And with that, splat—a shit stink of empathy lands on JD from some passing thought bird. Is it possible that the voices are themselves victims of trauma? Holy shit, no wonder they're so mean, Batman. They don't know who the fuck they are.

JD begins to take an interest in their daily habits, to listen deeply and ask questions. JD plies them with kindness, doling out tiny bits of affirmation like Smarties from a shaky pack. They teach the voices how to sing along to uplifting songs; Aretha Franklin's "I Say a Little Prayer" is the voices' favourite so far. JD is thrilled. Negotiations work intermittently; bounce-back bullying makes everything worse, but this R E S P E C T thing seems to be working. They ask to be named. JD doesn't rush into any offerings. They think long and hard about all that, with the deep caring of a parent naming a child.

JD finally decides on Joseph, Estelle, and Inez, after the three characters in Jean-Paul Sartre's play *No Exit*. It seems right to name them for the play that gave us the famous line "Hell is other people." JD reads the play to them every night and makes a dream come true that they didn't even know they had: they have become their own book club. The voices hungrily discuss Sartre's idea that human beings are "condemned to be free" because with freedom comes responsibility, and with responsibility comes existential anxiety.

JD tells them they believe Sartre when he wrote that human beings attempt to escape existential anxiety by giving up their freedom to others. In fact, that's what they think they did with the drinking and drugs, the bad marriage, the psychiatry, and maybe even the voices.

In the worst of it, says the newly named and astute Inez, "You've let us create meaning for you, which is a form of what Sartre refers to as 'bad faith.'" They all nod at once, and with the heaviness of that idea, JD passes out for a minute or two, suffering from a little bit of big-thought narcolepsy.

JD continues to read the voices *No Exit*, and they begin to take on the backstories and motivations of the characters, like actors rehearsing their roles. It doesn't take long before they are fighting amongst themselves. It doesn't take long before they begin to think of JD's head as a hell they are literally trapped in. The voices begin to cry out for freedom. JD decides to give them a little taste. They start small, suggesting the voices hop onto their shoulder for a moment at the park. Then JD moves to jumps, encouraging the voices to leap into the chair beside them at the library. Everything the voices experience outside JD seems to stun them into good behaviour. It's been a long time since they've been out. Are the voices ready for longer flights of freedom? JD can only hope. With all the audacity of a mediocre falconer, JD begins releasing their voice hawks to circle and swoop in the air above them before calling them back to safety.

JD continues to imagine the possibilities of this analogy of voices and birds, words and hawks, for a few years. Slowly, the voices go and come back. First for thirty seconds, then five minutes, then half an hour, and once, on a serendipitous day when their self-esteem was high and the weather conditions perfect, a whole day of release. They were at Jericho Beach when the tide was low.

They could almost see them go. Was it them or the wind rippling the water as the voices flew farther and farther from JD? Who can say? There were no witnesses.

Of course, JD is aware that they're guilty of anthropomorphic wishful thinking. They are thinking of the voices as existential wild birds of prey named Joseph, Estelle, and Inez. What's true is that JD is just fine with that. It's the best they can do at the time, and it seems to be working.

What JD really has to work hard to let go of is the fact that they don't know where the voices go when they're gone. When JD releases them one sunny afternoon from the window of their car, the voices do not return. JD is convinced that they are gone for good. They can only hope that it's not to nest in someone else's brain. They can only hope that their time together has evolved all of them into more compassionate entities.

JD feigns surprise when the voices come back to them three months later for what they say is a visit, but so far, they haven't left again. Did JD call them back with their own existential angst, or did they return to JD with theirs? JD will never know, but there is hope that JD and the voices are pointed more toward lives of good faith than bad—being in and of themselves, less delusion and more real. This is the story they tell to themselves, and it seems to make existence easier—this is just what is.

## The fantasies in no particular order

One of them never left. Many decades later, I return and find him behind the counter of the 7-Eleven on the side of the highway that runs through town. It's the only job he's ever had. He flirts with the high school girls sucking back Orange Crush and Coke-mixed Slurpees. "On the house, ladies, on the house."

I know it's him because of the way the hair on his knuckles is long and sweeps off to one side, two hands' worth of little Hitler hairdos. That and the chunky ring I don't remember. It's a signet ring: *WED*. I didn't remember that. His name tag reads *Walter*. I didn't remember that either. There is only a nickname—Ducky. It still bounces around my brain, like an echo in a cave.

"Ducky," a seemingly harmless name, nestled inside the more dangerous phrase, "Fuck her, Ducky, fuck her like a duck." But I may have made that part up. It's funny, so I can't be sure.

The teenaged girls in the 7-Eleven disperse like spent bubbles, and I slap two loonies down on the counter. Is Walter Ducky? I can't be sure and so I ask, "How about a scratch-and-win, Walter?" I point out the ticket I want. He pulls it out from the plastic cover, he's done it a million times before. I stare at him while scratching my ticket. I win $100,000 just like that. And then Walter, who may or may not be Ducky, is hopping up and down and he wants to take my picture because he's supposed to for the lottery foundation or something. Honestly, he's shrieking, like a little girl, like a stuck pig, like a little stuck-girl pig. And then I tell him, "Settle down, Ducky, settle down." He sneers, but it's comical, like a little part-pig, part-duck from a kids' book, who just happens to be working at 7-Eleven.

I tell him I'd like to ask him some questions. If he answers honestly, I'll give him my winning ticket. He turns his head away from me and smiles into one of the store's security cameras. I have no idea why.

I ask him if he remembers partying behind the grain elevators in high school.

"Yeah," he says, "like, all the time."

I ask him if he remembers him and his friends raping a girl from out of town in the back of a faded and battered red pickup truck. He tells me to get out of the store. I remind him that the truth will bring him $100,000. His lips slice a mean smile into his face.

He says, "Sure, sure, what the fuck. I remember that, sure."

I say, "I appreciate that, thank you." I leave the scratch-and-win ticket on the counter and walk out of the store. I don't tell him that the girl in the truck was me. Maybe, when he watches the security footage later, he'll figure that out. I also don't tell him that I switched the ticket he gave me with the one I had specially made. The ticket he thinks is a winner is fraudulent, counterfeit, bogus, likely to land him less in the green and more in a pot of boiling water.

—

One of them, the one who couldn't even bother to pull his pants down, the one who left zipper-track bruises on my groin and ripped the still-fuzzy hairs off my cunt, the one who never entered me who I think wasn't even hard, the last one, who said something like, "Don't worry, no one else is left." That one? He went on to become a prominent gay politician working fearlessly in the arena of human rights and was partly responsible for penning the UN resolution recognizing rape as a war crime.

The big one, the instigator, with his leather cowhide gloves on, had he done this before? That big belt and buckle, Kenmore. Removed with a Zorro-like flourish, let the games begin, slapped down on the bed of the truck. The sound of metal on metal.

That one who howled a bark, not worse than his bites. That one? He went on to run a farm in Saskatchewan. There he grew rapeseed, beat his wife and children, and became an alcoholic.

And one night when he was piss drunk and passed out in his old, long-dead, red pickup truck, his daughter—a hefty, handsome dyke who eventually took over running the farm (changing the crop over to lentils)—well, she pushed that long-dead, old, red pickup truck and the prick inside single-handedly into the slough. Her mother watched it sink from the kitchen window as she happened to be placing an apple pie on the ledge to cool.

—

The rest, two or three or four, I could never be sure, are an evil, Shiva-like blur of arms and legs all akimbo. Some things sometimes come into focus. Sport socks with red-and-blue stripes, brown pointy-toed cowboy boots. The smell of peppermint, bulging neck veins, young-voiced grunts, urging shouts, ball hats with rings of sweat around the rim, someone sucking air through his teeth, thin-wristed fists coming at me. All of them laughing like drunk actors in an amateur production of *The Iceman Cometh*. They rolled me out the back of the truck, mouthing the taste of dust and blood, into a dark that deepened as the headlights disappeared.

Anyway, those two or three or four ended up coming to a comedy show where I was performing. They came with their wives, who were all therapists, and they waited for me to finish my set and then called me over to their table. It seems that they'd all done their personal work, and we talked and drank club sodas with lime until 3 a.m. And those three or four men made amends to me, and their good wives all offered me free therapy for the rest of my days, but I thought that would be a little too weird, so I never called.

I have been accused of being too optimistic, but a fantasy is a fantasy, and that's such a light and hopeful-sounding word, isn't it? *Fantasy*. Of course, it can be paired with other menacing words, words like *revenge*. Revenge Fantasy. Okay. Fine. Those two or three or four, I can't be sure, organized the country's first and only Nude Harvesting Event. They had their peckers cut off in separate but gruesomely similar accidents that all involved copious amounts of Southern Comfort, naked dancing to the song "Ballroom Blitz," and John Deere combines just trying to make hay.

## If you leave her, can we come too

Remember that time you moved out, feeling as if you could never give her what she needed, and she could never love you the way you needed to be loved? I mean, come on, who can really love a loser? One of our greatest victories. You'd been with her sixteen years. You wouldn't even be here if she hadn't helped you with the resources for therapy and getting off all those drugs. We'd won. We convinced you, and we quote:

> *Garble garble me me me me ma. You sorry piece of shit. Hate you. Hate is the rule garbanzo bean misanthrope halitosis fucking dead meat fried on the grill. That one there looking at you like that fucking hates you. Bonkers fucking piece of shit. Ice-cold beer. Die die die. Blah blah blah fuck piss shit losing it man no way you can't even try you sorry piece of shit. You don't belong here, make room for someone else you fuck. Done. You are done. Fucking die you loser you fucking fucking loser.*

But then that fucking cat, Tay-O, was that his name? Against our wishes, that fucking cat got sick, six weeks after the severing. And the two of you decided to put down your pointy sticks and to keep all the rocks in your pockets. Remember? You two sat by the closet where that fucking cat was tucked in and dying, and recited that prayer you'd bumbled together, bits of bumper sticker wisdom picked up in dharma talks and books, nicknames for that fucking cat, gratitude for what he'd given you. The two of you called on Great Earth Mother, Gaia, Creator of the Universe, and some powerful and mysterious energy you feel acutely during manic episodes but have yet to name. You wanted to make sure you'd covered all your bases. You prayed for Tay-O the fucking cat to be free, you prayed that his energy would not be lost, you prayed that he would be safe and protected on his next journey. You called him Tay-O, Prince of the Universe and Tay-O the Wondercat. Sometimes that fucking cat would slap his tail and sit up like a proud lion, looking like nothing could possibly be wrong. Then he would lie down again, flattened out in pain, eyes half-open, seeing you maybe, but mostly seeing something or somewhere else.

Remember, when you couldn't see him suffer anymore, you took him to the vet so she could help him die. That vet who had done all the surgeries that had saved his life so many times before. Remember? When he fell from a window, nine storeys up, shattering his entire right side. Remember? And the two of you took turns nursing him back to health: ten surgeries, two blood transfusions. He ended up being a cat with 2.79 legs according to that vet.

You gave so much, so freely to that fucking cat. Too bad, so sad you couldn't give that way to each other. That day you two finally brought him in to die, that same vet said that mess of a prayer with you. She warned you that his eyes wouldn't close. She gave him a shot and you both held him, feeling his last exhale. It was creepy, those wonky, medicated eyes and then his life so suddenly gone. It was like a magic trick in reverse.

After that, you ended up on Acadia Beach. The skies were full of wildfire smoke, everything was grey and close. You didn't talk. At some point, you took off your shoes and socks and stood in the ocean for the first time that summer. She picked two thin oyster shells in her hands and made them tap dance on a flat grey rock. Heel toe. Heel toe. Shuffle shuffle. You were both present in that kind of awareness being with death brings. We were worried. We had faded to the sound of a radio on low in another room.

Remember you walked back up the hill from the beach and drove to the Naam for veggie burgers and sesame-baked fries with miso gravy. You ate that dinner in the apartment you used to share and ate some ice cream and she read you a poem by Marge Piercy called "Apologies." You tried not to read too much into that. We raised the volume. We wanted you to break open and spill out all your anger. How many times had we egged you on? Screamed you into blackout flashback trauma where you lost touch with the now and begged her to help you out of your own past. She was the one who pulled the trigger, reading that fucking poem, how could she not expect shots to be fired? But then you remembered you'd left her six weeks earlier, because you didn't want to do any more harm. You decided to stay quiet while we raged on in your head. You sat there and picked the skin off the top of your thumb until it bled. She brought you a Band-Aid and suggested you leave and that you could try to talk again tomorrow. You felt your chest filling with tears and knew the best thing you could do for everyone was to go and cry alone in your new apartment. You hugged, remember? There was pure love there, with no need, no agenda, fresh and dangerously healing.

Luckily for us, when you called in the morning, the grace of the previous day was gone. You had each picked up your pointy sticks again. Two years later, you still text each other that you love each other, every morning, and every night. You live apart and sometimes spend time together. You have agreed not to talk about even the tip of the iceberg. What remains below the surface does much better when it sleeps alone. You try to tell yourself that there are all kinds of love. All kinds. And come on, you're never truly alone. We'll always be here for you.

## Gone to pot

Schizo Susie calls one morning to say that her voices want to talk to my voices. Schizo Susie has taken up again with the green-headed charmer, Kush. She's fallen no birds and all bee's knees for the buzz buzz buzz of prescribed pot, made all okay-dokay with the doctor's stamp of approval. "Mary T wanna," she laughs, in that way stoned people do when they find something funny and don't give a shit whether you do or not. Schizo Susie says she's not going to be around for a while, she's had premonitions about going on a long trip, an extended vacation from reality.

She doesn't ask if I want to go, she knows I've tried pot to calm down but it only made me think I was Fred Flintstone. And when I started drawing black diamonds on long orange T-shirts, Yabba-Dabba-doing all day long and bowling trash cans down an alley, I knew it wasn't for me. Don't get me wrong, it was fun for a while, but unamused neighbours are quick to call the cops and I didn't want to take that ride again. Also, Schizo Susie knows I'm all aboard the sober train. Next station, Boring. Toot-toot! Schizo Susie disembarked from that old choo-choo a couple of months ago. She got off with all her baggage somewhere between stations and caught a ride on the legalized marijuana express. All we want for each other is to be happy, so I smiled and waved her goodbye. Unfortunately, she found the pot train too slow and within weeks was back on her transportation of choice, MDMA, a hot-air balloon piloted by a Velcro monkey afraid of the sun. Schizo Susie says she's having the time of her life and finds it all brilliant, absolutely brilliant. She tells me she'll never drink again, booze can slam you six feet under fast, but MDMA just keeps you adrift, head in the clouds, over and out. I mention that she always told me to stay away from any mind-altering substance. You take everything too seriously, little Polar Bear. Things have changed.

I hear the lighting of a spliff, the inhale, then the fuzzy sizzle of crystals dropped into water, followed by a rambling riff on what Schizo Susie is going to do when she's back from her trip: I'm going to organize pride parades for people with mental illnesses.

With Big Pharma sponsors. Think of the floats! But no, that's bonks, we should keep the focus on the people. Who will lead? The manics, obviously. The depressives will have to be somewhere in the middle, although I hear you, they belong at the end! But hear me. They'll need to be pushed along by the paranoid schizophrenics, who in turn will be corralled on either side by the borderline personalities. It will need to be a long parade. One out of four people in any big city are said to suffer from mental illness, so the parade will have to be for days, weeks maybe. The route will change; manics cannot be trusted to follow a plan, and those high-energy fuckers will never want it to end. We will all just have to wait till the manics swing into depression again, and then everyone will disperse and people who actually have lives can return to them. All the floats sponsored by the huge pharmaceutical companies can be adapted into temporary housing for those without. Some of the proud and crazy paraders of course will not recognize or be capable of believing that the parade is over. They will keep marching until they find another drum.

I hear the bubbling of a bong. I feel lonesome as a prairie.

Schizo Susie says, Put the voices on. Mine have some words of wisdom for yours. Write it down, Schizo Susie says, and say it to them every morning before you get up.

It's that good? I ask.

It's that good.

It's not that good. It's not all that bad. Her voices are stoned too. This is, at least, what I have time to scribble down:

*Game on. Level up. Rise from the dead. Shed the stigma. Self-destructive by nature? Then stay away from trees. Remember not to feed the beast of self-pity. Eat breakfast instead. Read this somewhere: be on the lookout for peculiar mental twists. Good luck with that. Also, same book: you are no longer alone. Bullshit, of course you are. Life wants to live. Does it? Oh, sorry, of course it does. Sit still in rooms stuffed with the stories of strangers who say they will love you until you love yourself.*

*Ha! Hold hands, take the serenity, courage, and wisdom and go-go gadget. Stay in touch. Ha! Remember*

*when you remembered phone numbers? Reread
Emerson's self-reliance. Alcohol and Drugs shut the
fuckers up, procured and prescribed. But do they? Here
we still are. Blah Blah Blah Blah Blah. Don't tell the tale
too many times, especially when you don't understand
the moral of the story. Like, remember that time you
tipped forward on the bridge and you felt someone grab
your belt and pull you back and when you looked, no
one was there? Invisible proof? A power greater than
yourself? God or your imagination? Same difference.
Make me a channel of this piece? Really? Why? Why
is not a spiritual question. Why not? We're trying to
help you out here. Are you grateful or what? Your
gratitude list is written in invisible ink. Ah, here it is.
For raccoons, aviation, matter, the memory of nicotine,
old Bic pen ads, babies, yo-yos, goalpost saves, zippers
that work, that Bozo the Clown plastic punching bags
were part of childhood, plasma, cotton briefs, vegan
doughnuts,* Hamlet, *xylophones, winter blues, hot dogs
at a ball game, the seven original sins, the faded orange
colour of Hot Wheels tracks, the word murmur, cats
that swim, men who punt.*

And then the sound of Schizo Susie crying. Her voices
stop lecturing mine, and I ask Schizo Susie if she's okay.
Of course not, she says, and then there is nothing but that
buzz buzz buzz that used to be there when someone hung
up a phone.

## Sink or swim

We try not to give them too much room to think about how different things might have been if the awful things that happened to them hadn't happened to them. For one thing, we wouldn't be here and maybe, just maybe, they would have been an easier person. Softer, more pleasant, volume set at three instead of nine, able to bloom where they were planted. A synchronized swimmer, precise and buff in a gorgeous outfit that complemented the others. Instead, we've made sure that they're often alone and flailing, look- ing crazed in an all-black onesie with those eye-popping goggles and slicked down in Vaseline to keep the imaginary jellyfish at bay. If they wander too far into the dry zone of *It is what it is*, we gleefully throw them back into the pool of warm self-pity pudding. Apparently, it's not an entire- ly uncomfortable feeling, suspended in the sticky goo, somewhere between sink and swim. What's true is that the longer they stay, the harder it is for them to get back out of the pool. And once they're in there, they can't help feel- ing that they're to blame for everything. Because because because we're shouting shit at them from poolside like the fucked-up coaches we are, "Give it up. You were there, things didn't just happen. You decided to stay or to believe everything was fine or to filter out certain facts or to not take the time to feel the twitch in your gut or the scratch of a scream itching its way up your throat, *Noooooo, don't let it go this way, you idiot!*"

We want them to drown in unanswerable questions. What am I really guilty of? How come I'm not over all this already? And our personal favourite, What the fuck is wrong with me?

Then they start thinking, "What kind of person lets themselves sleep in broken glass, and grab live wires that fried their insides, and doesn't think twice about letting people drug their brain and hurt them with words and punches and kicks and rock-hard peckers?"

Oh, they'll try to surface, to shake the chill of feeling like a victim, a martyr. We happily remind them how insecure and pathetic they are, waiting, still waiting for a prince by any other name to rescue them from their pain. "Poor you," we scream, "trapped in the deep-end dungeon for the crime of not understanding your part in things. Why won't anyone relieve you of this pain?" When that magic elixir or person or lover or job or vacation or lucky break or pitch-perfect circumstance doesn't show, they rage, wear themselves out. We never let them even dream that perhaps they could become more responsible for themselves. We tell them how hard that would be. I mean, they don't even have a mighty steed or a trusty sword. Swaths of calendar days have been X'd out due to their arduous, slow-moving, lopsided, forward crawl toward the place they were last seen standing. And of course, their little me/thees and she/hers and they/thems have all been to therapy. The kinds that encourage redirecting the rage toward those who deserve it, or forgiving others, or finding where the feelings from the past live in the body and freeing them to get up and go, or practising daily affirmations of what you're doing right today, or balancing the masculine and feminine energies, re-parenting your inner child, learning to love yourself. They've read a lot of self-help books. (It kills us that it's called self-help. If they're buying other people's books, aren't they hoping that *they'll* help them?)

In the past few years, there has been a troubling trend. Daily, they stop swimming and allow themselves to sink to the bottom of the pool. Then they sit and focus, saying over and over to themselves, *"Right now, it's like this and I care. Right now, it's like this and I care."*

The self-pity pool only has a shallow end now and they have gained some sort of skill that seems to make the swimming easier. We are hoping this is just a phase.

## Losing my marbles; Or, why the voices wish I wouldn't meditate

A marble, rattling around my mind, falls out of my ear? My nose? My vagina? My asshole? I can't say for certain; I missed the moment. Wherever it emerged, the marble was heavy, dense with the weight of obsessive thinking, tightly layered with foggy, half-formed ideas wrapped around one another, fragmented sentences, a lot of question marks, even more exclamation marks, angry emojis, crying emojis, a long list of names crossed out with red ink. All condensed over the years by the heat of self-righteous anger. It left a three-inch dent in my apartment floor.

Other marbles begin to fall out of me, one by one at first. They drop with little cartoon sounds — Blam! Blam! Blam! They roll all over my nearly empty apartment. Then the marbles start pouring out. In an audible sleight of sound, BLAM! steals the letter *E* from the front of the Echo ricocheting off my walls. The now-silent *E* slinks in low self-esteem to the back of BLAM! Less comic now, the marbles land loudly with an affirmative BLAME! BLAME! BLAME!

When I am up to my neck in marbles, the floor collapses. I fall through apartments 321, 221, 121, the amenities room, and P1 and P2 in the underground parking. I think briefly of Kazuo Ishiguro's *The Unconsoled* when I hear someone playing piano. I continue to plummet down into the silty clay that lies under Vancouver. I can feel my body leaving me, gently combusting, slowly disappearing.

Soon, I am sawdust. This seems wrong to me. Shouldn't I be stardust? I shouldn't be surprised to learn that I am made of wood. I have always known, I was never a real boy, eh Geppetto? Then poof, just like that, I am reduced to ashes. My body is gone but not the sensation of falling. I descend through the North American Plate and the Juan de Fuca Plate to land on a fault line marked—My. My Fault. One of the marbles stops long enough to whisper to me, *Not the trauma itself, that's not your fault, but how you treat others when you're triggered. You have to take responsibility for your behaviour when you hurt someone. No exceptions. In this way you will find some healing.*

The marbles keep coming, some hit me in the head, adding injury to insight, others fall past me, to be consumed by the earth's fiery core, or maybe to form a huge pile of lost marbles that wait to be summoned back to sanity by a whistle only the mad know.

I don't want to think about what the marble said to me, so I start to replay scenes from an episode I watched last weekend of the National Geographic series *One Strange Rock*. I learned about an organism that lived some four billion years ago that is thought to be the origin of all living things. All living things! Scientists have dubbed it LUCA—Last, Universal, Common, Ancestor. This organism is still found in some hydrothermal vents at the bottom of the oceans. LUCA. LUCA. LUCA. What a miracle. None of us humans would be here without the exact combination of water, energy, and sawdust, oops, I mean stardust, a.k.a. carbon.

LUCA. Something bumps my mind from this majestic knowing into the lyrics of Suzanne Vega's 1987 song "Luka." A slight change in spelling, but I follow the drift.

My name is Luka
I live on the second floor
I live upstairs from you
Yes, I think you've seen me before

I feel ashamed to know for certain that I will remember these lyrics for eternity and have already forgotten what the acronym LUCA stands for. There is so much worthy of knowing that has been paved over with pop songs. Pop goes the pop song when you hear the Buddhist teacher on the guided meditation you're listening to say, "Where are you right now?"

## Brick and Goose

Last summer, that Canada goose, alone and padding awkwardly over the grooved and fitted bricks on Olympic Plaza in downtown Calgary. Possibly over the bricks with our family names on them, purchased by my dad to mark his support of the 1988 Calgary Olympics. We are in the cross-country section, all laid out in a row of red dusty brick. I caught up with the goose and saw a shard of brown, possibly beer bottle glass, poking out from the side of its beak. "Oh, little buddy, don't eat glass." I stop to consider how I might pull the glass out of the goose's beak. A beak closed for now over top and bottom rows of spiky barbs. I have never been bitten, but still I am shy. I don't know what to do, so I pull out my notebook, maybe I'll find some instructions there to help me? I don't find anything pertinent. The goose flies away. I write:

> This is one of those moments, where I feel as if most of
> the world lives in an annual report and I live in a poem.
> A poem that's not written yet, a poem where fractured
> ideas fall all around me and ask to be lined up, to give
> them meaning and rhythm and nuance and beauty.
> Brick and Goose. This sounds more like a pub I used to
> drink in and maybe got kicked out of? Brick and Goose.
> These things have appeared together and want my

*attention. The thing with the bricks is, seeing them like that, and knowing that's the only place you could see all my family's names together until we all signed the guest book at my dad's funeral a year ago. And even then, the names aren't the same; some of us married, some of us changed in other ways. Here's the thing, about the other thing, the goose with broken beer bottle glass in his beak? It took me to that day last July, when I was phoned and told my dad was in a coma, self-induced by swallowing all his pills. Maybe when he was drunk and not knowing what he was doing. Maybe he was just in that much pain. Who can say? I was in Vancouver and didn't know what to do. Should I get myself to Calgary? Should I wait and see if this was as serious as it sounded? There had been so many near misses. With an alcoholic parent, every close call you get moves you further and further away from any sense of urgency. I went for a walk around my neighbourhood. I asked for a sign that he would make it to the other side. I wasn't sure who I was asking or what I meant by the other side. A moment later, in the middle of a hot summer afternoon, a small V of geese flew above me. Geese had been his thing. He loved to point out a goose whenever he could, until he cooked his own.*

## Tender is the Dyke

Before depression is a dog, it's cigarette smoke. Blown in your face at night when you're asleep, so the detector doesn't go off. You wake up annoyed and, strangely, wanting more. There is nothing there except the sounds of you coughing your anxieties awake, trying to catch your breath, caught in a panic of airless heaves. Your heart knows to hide. A good heart can shift and jimmy itself under a shoulder blade. You didn't know that? You'll think it's a knot in your muscles. You'll think it's from tension. There have, after all, been more than a few bad days. Your heart stays hidden and night after night the cigarette smoke will come. On the morning you can't seem to get out of bed, a big dog will be sitting on your chest. A cigarette turned completely to ash will hang from its lips. The dog will smile or say *huh* or maybe *boo*; it depends what kind of dog you get. The grey ash will fall into your eyes and your ears and your mouth and your nose. You will forget that there was ever anything to see or hear or taste or smell.

This crushing and suffocating place, like the kind of bar you don't want to end up in, unless you're looking for a fight, is where Janice cries out for you. She is three, and sits in front of an open fridge, learning to use a bottle opener. This is one of those family stories that's told again and again, like it's something funny. But Janice is shivering and her father is supposed to be there, watching her. He's behind a closed door with someone giggling who is not her mother. Maybe this is in the party room in an apartment they lived in when Janice was young? Her mother is upstairs maybe? Making food for the party? Janice has opened several beers and taken sips, so the story goes.

She calls for you, JD, every time that big dog shows up to blow smoke in your face. You refused to hear Janice for years. And when you finally did, you were surprised when she said, *I need you to not forget me, I need you to be as gentle as you can to me. It's me you need to take care of.* Never say never. Tender is the Dyke who learns to love the lonely little girl who remains a part of them.

## Even after all these years

A bright, low moon beams its way through a gap in the trees. The light interrogates the room, and you wake in terror. You tell yourself, *It's the moon, go back to sleep.* And even though you try not to lie to yourself, you can't always be sure you're telling the truth. The moon is never just a moon, is it? Those of us inside your head offer another explanation. It's not the moon, it's a searchlight. They've found you, the ones who know you're really crazy, and they've come to take you away. Ha ha hee hee. You move your hand in a circle over your heart. Tenderness has always confused us. The earth does what it does, and the moon glides back into the darkness. We do not come any closer. You have come back to the here and now, recognizing us as the delusions we are. Your heart slows to the beat of a lucky human drifting off again into sleep.

## What if everything's beautiful?

Like when you take off in a plane and it's raining, and all that rain gets swept over the wings, and there is so much water that everything below passes by in a blurry whirl until the word *MOTEL* appears in bright-yellow letters on the roof of a building.

And that older, chubby white guy squeezed into an apron two sizes too small who works for the Korean lady in her restaurant and wears a hairnet and always reminds me when he serves my bibimbap that the bowl is still hot, *like, cast-iron hot, because it actually is, because it's still cooking your food, that's how cast-iron hot that bowl is.*

And what about Harry? Harry who sat across from me in the Korean lady's restaurant, listening to me talk about trying to reconnect with my mom, who is sick again, and how it feels like it's all a movie that I should be in, but I can't get into the movie because the only people who can be in the movie have been in the movie all this time, so it's not my movie. So, I just have to watch, and most of the time I feel okay with that, and other times I feel so guilty and useless about not being a part of the movie all this time that maybe I'll explode like a bag of microwave popcorn and so what, no harm done, everybody loves popcorn, right? I mean, would you trust anybody who didn't like popcorn?

And Harry is definitely beautiful because he just does

this little twitch of a smile, and he doesn't even ask any questions because he knows I just need to ramble, and he keeps listening as I stretch the metaphor like an old elastic to its breaking point. "I wasn't even asked to audition for the part of the daughter beside the bedside because anybody who's anybody knows I'd make a terrible daughter by the bedside because I've always made a terrible daughter anywhere else and that makes me feel really shitty sometimes because it's true and what's also true is that most of the time it makes me feel deliriously relieved. The least they could do is give me one little scene. How hard could that be? I ride by on a Harley, wave goodbye, and the smoke swirls up and out of the exhaust pipes and spells *I love you forever Mom*, and by the time the smoke disappears, so have I."

"That could be beautiful," said Harry, "with the right director." And then Harry, a man small enough to shop in the boys' department, lets his big brown eyes fill up with just enough water to make them look all glassy, like deeply concerned marbles. He's right on the edge of a cry as the sentences finally stop falling out of my mouth. And maybe because I've stopped or maybe because he thinks about the part with the motorcycle again, Harry laughs and I do too, and then we sit and eat our bibimbap and say nothing for quite a while.

I love Harry, and if I were younger and shorter and straight, I might even sleep with Harry, maybe even in the motel by the airport with the big bright-yellow letters on the roof. But I'm not any of those things and that's probably better for everyone concerned.

## 4 5 6 7

JD is in their parents' backyard again, two days after having bibimbap with Harry, six years since the last of the ice age melted away, ten years since the last happy story told of their parents peeling apples in the yard, and eight months since their father died. JD is here in Calgary for work, but also because this is the day of their parents' wedding anniversary. Today would have marked sixty-five years. Some relatives have brought over Chicken on the Way, deep-fried drumsticks and breasts with fries and corn fritters. It was the choice for picnics in the early days of their parents' marriage. A picture is taken of everyone except their father in front of the apple tree. The same spot where their parents took a picture every year for their anniversary. Usually, the boughs are stippled with blossoms, but it's been a cold May. Nobody eats much and then they all do a few things in the yard. JD repots a lily and pulls some weeds, shaking off a shiver of fear that the ghost of their father will appear and tell them that they're doing it wrong. It is so much calmer without him. JD realizes what's happening is ordinary, still a concept they have trouble recognizing. Psychiatrists used to ask how they were feeling on a scale of 1 to 10. It took them years to understand they didn't know what a 4, 5, 6, or 7 felt like. JD wants to stay here, to feel this moment as is, but they can sense tendrils of the past wrapping round their ankles, threatening to pull them down. JD still wants all their memories to fall in line, to make sense of the present. They want to feel confident that they will always be the same, like a Big Mac from McDonald's—first two all-beef patties, then special sauce, lettuce, cheese, pickles, onion, and finally a sesame seed bun. When will they learn, memories are mom-and-pop shops, not international restaurant chains.

JD doesn't need to be a figment of Miriam Toews's imagination anymore to be here in their parents' backyard, but they still rely on made-up things to get them through. It is Joshua Dandelion, pulling weeds out from around the pansies, who whispers to Janice, "Maybe you didn't tell your mom what happened because you knew she couldn't bear it, not with everything else she had to deal with. She didn't choose not to hear, you chose not to tell."

Joshua Dandelion recalls the old adage from the Big Book of Alcoholics Anonymous, *We're only as sick as our secrets.* But maybe, in families steeped in the perpetual state of crisis that alcoholism creates, there is a necessary triaging of secrets—a sorting of wounds into degrees of urgency, a lining up of ambulances that may take many years to arrive. It is no one's fault. It is just what is. Sometimes there is not enough care to go around. JD smiles at these thoughts that have come to them the way they do, like shooting stars out of the disordered cosmos. All these years later, when the veins have started to pop up on the backs of their hands, like the roots of poplars that surface through the grass as trees grow older. Only now do these thoughts arrive. JD wants to write everything down right away, so they don't forget, but feels strange about pulling a notebook out from their back pocket with all the relatives here in their parents' yard.

Later, when everyone leaves, JD will go for a walk by themselves up a hill that they like in a neighbourhood called Bridgeland. They'll get a vegan ice cream, probably lemon saffron. While JD waits in line for their cone at Made by Marcus, they'll have the time and the space to scribble a few things down. Ice cream cone in hand, they'll walk up the hill, where you can see the mountains in one direction and the prairies in the other. They have always liked this in-between land of the foothills, dusty and scrappy. Also, there are dandelions on this hill, in patches of their own and mixed in with the ground-covering yellows of buffalo beans.

And those huge clouds that gather in Calgary, flat on the bottom and growing quickly, clouds piling on top of each other, like a stack of Mallomar cookies after you've eaten the chocolate off.

JD writes something else in their notebook before they walk back down the hill—an incomplete idea that maybe they'll come back to later.

*I wish we could go by pro-verbs instead of pro-nouns.*
*We could pick new ones every day if we needed to.*
*Would this help us make more sense to each other?*
*Hi, my name is Joshua Dandelion, I prefer JD. My*
*pro-verbs are grief and wonder. You?*

## And so

There are memories that can be called home like loose, hungry dogs, and there are ones that come all Lou Reed-like, knocking on your door. There are the ones that come without warning, ranging from gentle breezes across the back of the neck to T-bone crashes at unmarked railway crossings.

There are sayings—a flood of memories, a blast from the past, memories are golden, or something like that. And if you lose everything, at least you have your memories. There is talk of good memories and bad memories, and much opinion about which ones should be kept and which ones should be tossed into the trash to be hauled away, burned, and buried. Many of us are unable to do this kind of sorting into good/bad. Some of us are memory hoarders; believing that some of this will be of use down the road, we keep everything. There are, of course, the sorts of memories that can never be vouched for; there will be no search-party flashlights finding anything beyond the shadow of a doubt. One can go mad trying to coax these lurking memories out of the dark. What is called insanity might be nothing more than being lost in thought, forever gone down down down some unending tunnel, looking for some piece of some-thing that happened that, when found, will make sense of everything.

I have stopped looking for the missing pieces, but I do not regret going into the dark to see what I could see. I have decided to believe that what happened when I was just a girl of thirteen happened. I have decided that it doesn't matter if anyone else believes me.

I have decided that even if I can't be exactly sure about anything that happened, I mean *really* happened, I can, somehow, if only from the whispering that comes from my bones, know that it did happen. What has my imagination tried to solidify? What grainy pictures were actually taken by my brain at the scene? I can't be sure. But perhaps there is payback for living with the voices all these years. They are my proof. They are here to remind me that something catastrophic did indeed go down, that something violent and unfair happened to me and changed the way my brain works. Experiences were forced upon me that broke things in me that would have served me better if they'd been left whole. I have decided to believe because by not believing, I could never do what needed to be done.

And that was to get angry at what happened, to make it all about me for a time so that the rage could be directed back into the past instead of at the people directly in front of me. To let that anger burn bright and hot and sometimes, yes, out of control and to finally die down into a small, heart-held fire that will always be with me. After the anger came the grief, first in unfathomable waves that pushed me to the bottom, nearly drowning me, then turned me around and around in deep blues of sadness that had a chokehold on hope for years. And then?

Out of the dark, still dripping with salty water, still a little on fire, walking into the larger world. And then?

Finding myself with something to say.

# Acknowledgements

With gratitude to Kacey Rohl, Jessica Bolland, Smudge, Buddy, Buttons and Bows, Kadoodles, Doots, KMER, Sport, Jessica Messica, MVP Beth Sweeney, Adrienne Wong, Larry Kwok, Jessica Schneider, Jordan Baylon, Arty, E. Sweeney, Zsuzsi Gartner, Col Cseke, Dana Ayotte, Andrew McIlroy, Sable Sweetgrass, Beth Gibson, Peter Smith, Mary Stancavage, Lindsay Eales, Tanya Marquardt, Jean Marie Lillian, Lili Robinson, Jutta Treverianus, Dani Feko, Dave Deaveau, Daniel Martin, Emmy Nordstrom, John Sweet, all the good folks at Goose Lane Editions, Dania Sheldon, Natalie Meisner, Mark Leiren-Young, Ivan E. Coyote, and Fay Nass.

JD Derbyshire (they/them) is a Vancouver-based comedian, theatre maker, writer, and mad activist whose work examines mental health, neurodiversity, queerness, and gender exploration. Derbyshire has toured Canada as a stand-up comedian and solo performer; has written over twenty plays that have been produced by companies in Victoria, Calgary, Toronto, and Vancouver; and co-hosts the mental health podcast *Mad Practice*. Their play *Certified*, which served as partial inspiration for *Mercy Gene*, turns the audience into a mental health review board to determine Derbyshire's sanity by the end of the show. *Certified* won two Jessie Richardson Theatre Awards in Vancouver and was described by the *Georgia Straight* as "a testament to a dynamic performance and delicate storytelling." *Mercy Gene* is Derbyshire's first novel.